Farmer Giles of Ham

FARMER GILES
OF HAM

Ægidii Ahenobarbi Julii Agricole de Hammo
Domini de Domito
Aule Draconarie Comitis
Regni Minimi Regis et Basilei
mira facinora et mirabilis
exortus

or in the vulgar tongue

The Rise and Wonderful Adventures of
Farmer Giles, Lord of Tame,
Count of Worminghall
and King of
the Little Kingdom

BY

J.R.R. TOLKIEN

Embellished by
PAULINE BAYNES

Edited by
CHRISTINA SCULL
WAYNE G. HAMMOND

Houghton Mifflin Company
BOSTON NEW YORK

Text of *Farmer Giles of Ham* copyright © 1949 by George Allen & Unwin Ltd.

Copyright © restored 1996 by The Estate of J.R.R. Tolkien, assigned

1997 to The J.R.R. Tolkien Copyright Trust

Previously unpublished material by J.R.R. Tolkien

copyright © 1999 by the Tolkien Trust

Introduction and Notes copyright © 1999 by HarperCollins*Publishers*

Map of the Little Kingdom copyright © 1999 by Pauline Baynes

www.hmhco.com

ISBN 0-618-00936-1
CIP data is available.

Printed in the United States of America

21 22 23 24 25 LSB 19 18 17 16 15

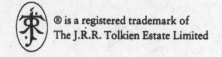

To C. H. Wilkinson

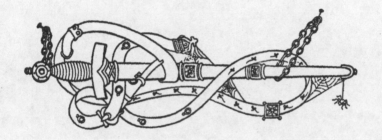

Contents

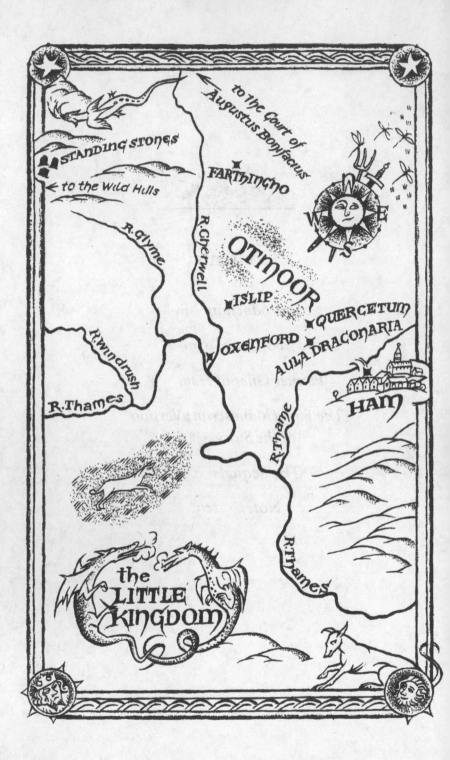

Introduction

FARMER GILES OF HAM, like *Roverandom*, was invented by J.R.R. Tolkien to entertain his children, and was originally an oral tale. Once set on paper it grew in length and complexity over a period of some twenty years, its main text progressing from a manuscript to four typescripts and galley proofs before it was published at last in 1949. Most of these papers are preserved in the Department of Special Collections and University Archives, Marquette University Libraries, in Milwaukee, Wisconsin.

Tolkien's eldest son, John, has recalled that the tale was first told when the family was caught in a rainstorm after a picnic and took shelter under a bridge. This event can be neither dated nor located with any precision. But almost certainly a story inspired by the country around Oxford would have been told after the Tolkiens moved to that city from Leeds in early 1926, and the style and tone of its earliest written version are closer to *Roverandom* as it was first written down, probably at the end of 1927, than to the earliest extant texts of *The Hobbit*, a comparatively mature work, from around 1930.

This first version of *Farmer Giles*, written by hand on twenty-six pages, was much shorter and simpler than the book published in 1949. It is narrated by 'Daddy', who interrupts the story for questions near the beginning and at the end. Moreover he puts it in a personal context for his audience: 'if he [the giant] had trodden on *our* garden', 'if he had bumped into *our* house'. Though there is some play with words, most of the philological jokes and scholarly allusions that make the 1949 text so notable are missing. These include, for example, all of the Latin references, the texts of the two letters to Giles from the King, and most of the nomenclature. The only names given in the manuscript are *Giles*, *Ham*, *Tailbiter*, and *Worminghall*. The dragon, Giles' dog, and the King are all nameless. The characters of Giles, the King, and the dragon are already quite developed, though not as deep as in later versions. The dog and the blacksmith are still very rudimentary, and the miller is hardly hinted at. Nor is there any mention of Giles having a wife. Little attention is paid to the journey back with the dragon's treasure: Giles does not worry how to secure the dragon at night, and there are no 'likely lads'. The story is given no historical background, though it seems to take place in the Middle Ages. The locale is also vague – 'the giant lived a long way from here, a long way from anywhere where people lived' – until the end when 'Daddy' explains that Giles took the surname Worming and built a fine hall in Ham, after which the village was called Worminghall, which can still be found on the map (a few miles from Oxford). The story ends with 'Daddy' declaring that its real hero was the Grey Mare.

A second version, the first typescript, departed from the manuscript in only a few small but notable respects. Now the tale was told by the 'family jester' (not a name by which Tolkien was known, as far as his children recall); at the end he asks his listeners who they think was the real hero of the story, 'and there were quite a number of different answers'. The events of *Farmer Giles* are now definitely placed in the past – 'that giant lived a long time ago', 'in those days and in those places it was the only kind of gun there was; people preferred bows and arrows, and used gunpowder mostly for fireworks' – and distances and time are now compressed. For example, Giles' magic sword leaps out of its sheath if a dragon is within two miles, not a hundred miles as before. Like the manuscript, the first typescript cannot be dated precisely, but it was in existence by the early or mid-1930s. Simonne d'Ardenne, a Belgian scholar whose thesis Tolkien supervised, translated the first typed version into French, most likely when she lodged with the Tolkien family in Oxford in 1932–3, but before November 1937 when Tolkien mentioned the translation in a letter.

In late 1936 George Allen & Unwin accepted *The Hobbit* for publication, and on the strength of it asked Tolkien to submit other children's stories he had written. In response he sent his picture-book *Mr. Bliss*, his story of the dog Roverandom, and *Farmer Giles of Ham*. Stanley Unwin, the head of the firm, asked his eleven-year-old son for his opinion. Rayner Unwin's report on *Farmer Giles of Ham*, dated 7 January 1937, was enthusiastic:

> One day a giant got lost on the mountains and wandered down to the town of Ham, Farmer Giles saw him and fired his blunderbuss at him, the giant thought it was knats [gnats] stinging him and decided he was walking in the wrong direction so he turned back. The king heard of this and gave him a sword. Some time afterwards a dragon came into the neighbourhood and Farmer Giles was forced to fight him, the dragon was mortally afraid of the sword and submitted to giving the farmer a lot of money. This money never arrived so some knights and this Giles went to kill him, he killed the knights but when he saw Farmer Giles' sword he gave him the money and came to the Farmer's house as a pet but when the king came to claim the money he went back faster than he came!
>
> This is a well written and amusing book, it should make a good book and might be published with 'Roverandom' in one volume.
>
> It needs some illustrations, perhaps the author's own? This book should appeal to every English boy or girl.

However, the success of *The Hobbit*, published in September 1937, convinced Allen & Unwin that Tolkien's next book for them should be a sequel, more about hobbits; or failing that, *Farmer Giles of Ham* with other stories like it, for Stanley Unwin felt that the one tale was not in itself enough to make a book. In December 1937 Tolkien chose to write the sequel, and began *The Lord of the Rings*; but by the end of July 1938 it was clear that he could not finish his 'new Hobbit' in time for the Christmas season as his publisher had hoped. On 24 July he offered an alternative: 'the only line I have', he told Allen & Unwin,

> is 'Farmer Giles' and the Little Kingdom (with its capital at Thame). I rewrote that to about 50% longer, last January,

and read it to the Lovelace Society in lieu of a paper 'on' fairy stories. I was very much surprised at the result. It took nearly twice as long as a proper 'paper' to read aloud; and the audience was apparently not bored – indeed they were generally convulsed with mirth. But I am afraid that means it has taken on a rather more adult and satiric flavour. Anyway I have not written the necessary two or three other stories of the Kingdom to go with it! [*Letters of J.R.R. Tolkien*, p. 39]

The Lovelace Society was an essay club at Worcester College, Oxford. Tolkien had addressed its members, by invitation, on the evening of 14 February 1938. To prepare his 'paper' he entered a few changes on the first typescript of *Farmer Giles of Ham*, but for the most part revised and enlarged the story in the process of making a new typescript, now lost (but mentioned in correspondence until early 1949). He called it 'The Legend of Worming Hall', according to the secretary of the Lovelace Society. The minutes book of the Society, preserved at Worcester College, contains a brief description of Tolkien's presentation and confirms his claim that his audience was amused. When he finished, it was judged that his story allowed neither criticism nor discussion – a compliment to the author, maybe, but by then the hour was late.

Tolkien had the revised story professionally retyped by the Academic Copying Office in Oxford. This typescript was not only much longer than the previous extant version, but much more sophisticated. At first it was labelled *The Lord of Tame, Dominus de Domito: A Legend of Worminghall*, but this title was deleted and Tolkien returned to *Farmer Giles of Ham* as on the earliest drafts. In the revised version he introduced most of the proper names, jokes, and allusions that enliven the book, for example the 'Four Wise Clerks of Oxenford' and their definition of *blunderbuss*. The characters are now more fully developed, including the dog (now called Garm), the dragon Chrysophylax Dives, the miller, and the blacksmith (Fabricius Cunctator or 'Sunny Sam'); and Giles' wife, Agatha, appears for the first time. The story is set 'a very long time ago, when this island was still happily divided into many kingdoms'. Ham is now the precursor of the modern town of Thame, and *Worminghall* the vernacular form of *Aula Draconaria*, the name of the house built by Giles on the spot where he and Chrysophylax first met. 'Daddy' and the 'Family Jester' happily have disappeared, but the author still occasionally intrudes to speak directly to the reader ('If you think his name was unsuitable I can only say that it was not').

On 31 August 1938 Tolkien submitted the new typescript to Allen & Unwin to consider, noting that 'a good many folk have found it very diverting' (*Letters*, p. 40). After several months he had no response, and in the new year inquired further, most pointedly on 10 February: 'Did *Farmer Giles* in the enlarged form meet with any sort of approval? . . . Is it worth anything? . . . I just wonder whether this local family game played in the country just round us is more than silly' (*Letters*, p. 43). He continued to promote the book to Allen & Unwin through the end of 1939, as an interim substitute for *The Lord of the Rings* which was progressing slowly. After that, during the war years, there was little discussion of the matter, and no resolution, until Tolkien raised the question again in July 1946.

Farmer Giles was now read for the publisher by David Unwin (the author 'David Severn'), who found it 'delicious' and 'a real joy'. The only concern remained its length, brief even after its enlargement for the Lovelace Society, and what works by Tolkien might accompany it to make a book long enough to sell reasonably for six shillings. Tolkien still had nothing finished that his publisher thought suitable, and his academic duties allowed him no leisure to provide other stories in the same line, even if he had felt inclined to write them. 'The heart has gone out of the Little Kingdom,' he had remarked in 1945, referring to the countryside around Oxford, 'and the woods and plains are aerodromes and bomb-practice targets' (*Letters*, p. 113).

At last Allen & Unwin decided to publish *Farmer Giles of Ham* alone, without any sequels or other stories, and to make it a sufficiently long book by adding illustrations. Tolkien now reviewed the latest typescript and made 'a good many alterations, for the better (I think and hope) in both style and narrative' (5 July 1947, *Letters*,

p. 119). Some of the changes were so substantive that he replaced seven of the original sheets by retyping on the reverse. He deleted some of the remaining intrusive remarks by the narrator, and he now added, among other points of interest, the description of the giant brushing aside elms like tall grasses and leaving his 'best copper pot' on the fire, the parson's remarks on the letters inscribed on Tailbiter and its sheath, and his suggestion that Giles take some rope when hunting the dragon. The Middle Kingdom was now so named, its court placed some twenty leagues distant from Ham; and Giles' unfortunate cow was now called Galathea.

Around this time Tolkien also added a 'foreword', which he developed through several drafts. The earliest of these are written on the reverse of Oxford University notices dated October 1946, and together with early typescripts are preserved in the Bodleian Library, Oxford. Later versions are in the Marquette University Archives. In fact it is a mock foreword, as *Farmer Giles of Ham* is a mock medieval heroic adventure, indeed one *jeu d'esprit* added to another. Tolkien pretends to be the editor and translator of an ancient text – a pose he would later adopt in the first edition of *The Lord of the Rings* (1954) and in *The Adventures of Tom Bombadil* (1962) – and presents it as true, more or less, 'a legend, perhaps, rather than an account' of the history of the Little Kingdom.

Many who have written about *Farmer Giles of Ham* have interpreted its foreword as a satirical extension by Tolkien of his British Academy lecture, *Beowulf: The Monsters and the Critics* (1936; reprinted in Tolkien, *The Monsters and the Critics and Other Essays*, 1983). In that landmark work he criticized the critics who approached *Beowulf* only as a historical document, not as a poem worthy of attention for its literary merits. 'The illusion of historical truth and perspective, that has made *Beowulf* seem such an attractive quarry,' he wrote, 'is largely a product of art. The author has used an instinctive historical sense . . . but he has used it with a poetical and not an historical object.' *Farmer Giles* of course is wholly a product of art; but its editor as portrayed in the foreword, akin to certain critics of *Beowulf*, is interested only in the glimpse the text affords of the history of Britain and the origin of certain place-names, not with the story as a story. Some readers, he admits, 'may find the character and adventures of its hero attractive in themselves', implying by his dismissive tone that he himself does not. Moreover he accepts as historical fact the sometimes bogus history of Britain as told by Geoffrey of Monmouth and repeated in later fiction such as *Sir Gawain and the Green Knight*.

This interpretation of the foreword may or may not reflect Tolkien's intent. In any case it is important to remember that the foreword is satirical, and that it was an afterthought, not written until the story proper had been in existence for many years. Put another way, *Farmer Giles of Ham* itself was not written from the same point of view. Although the foreword places the events of *Farmer Giles* more narrowly in time than does the story itself, between the end of the third century (the time of King Coel) and the early sixth century (the rise of the Seven Kingdoms of the English), this is beside the point as far as the reader should be concerned. *Farmer Giles of Ham* is meant to belong to no particular era of history, beyond 'those days, now long ago, when this island was still happily divided into many kingdoms' (p. 9). Its 'medieval' setting is merely an appropriate background for a tale of dragons and knights, against which Tolkien places anachronisms for humorous effect, of which the 'pact of non-aggression' between Giles and the dragon (p. 78) is perhaps the most glaringly modern. As Tolkien confessed to his friend Naomi Mitchison, *Farmer Giles*

was I fear written very light-heartedly, originally of a 'no-time' in which [seventeenth-century] blunderbusses or anything might occur. Its slightly donnish touching up, as read to the Lovelace Soc[iety], and as published, makes the Blunderbuss rather glaring – though not really worse than all medieval treatments of Arthurian matter. But it was too embedded to be changed, and some people find the anachronisms amusing. I myself could not forgo the quotation [describing the blunderbuss] . . . from the Oxford Dictionary. . . . But in the Isle of Britain in archeological fact there can have been nothing in the least like a fire-arm. But neither was there fourteenth century armour [in the days of Farmer Giles]. [18 December 1949, *Letters*, p. 133]

Tolkien sent a rough copy of the foreword, together with his newly revised typescript, to Allen & Unwin in July 1947. The book was then delayed for more than a year. Since Tolkien had himself made no pictures for *Farmer Giles of Ham*, he suggested that they be drawn by Milein Cosman, a young artist his daughter Priscilla felt should be given a chance. Cosman was slow to produce the specimen pictures requested, however, and those she eventually delivered in January and July 1948 pleased neither Tolkien nor Allen & Unwin. Cosman was dismissed (she went on to have a successful career), and the commission given instead to Pauline Baynes, whose mock-medieval cartoons in her portfolio caught Tolkien's eye. Baynes at once entered into the spirit of the book, and with typical energy and skill produced more line drawings than requested, as well as two colour plates. She completed most of the work by early March 1949. Tolkien wrote to Allen & Unwin that he was pleased with Baynes' art 'beyond even the expectations aroused by the first examples. They are more than illustrations, they are a collateral theme. I showed them to my friends whose polite comment was that they reduced my text to a commentary on the drawings' (*Letters*, p. 133). In 1976 Baynes painted new cover art for the second edition of *Farmer Giles*, details from which have been used on the cover of the present book, and in 1980 drew new full-page illustrations for a reprint in the Tolkien collection *Poems and Stories*. For this anniversary edition Pauline Baynes has contributed a map of the Little Kingdom, thus marking fifty years of association with *Farmer Giles of Ham*.

In late 1948 Tolkien made, for the use of the printer, a fresh typescript with only a handful of emendations, mostly of typographical errors, and in the process entered corrections retroactively on the previous typescript. He made a few more changes at the eleventh hour on the printer's galley proofs, most notably removing a reference to the giant's boots when Pauline Baynes delivered two fine drawings of a giant with bare feet.

Farmer Giles of Ham was published at last on 20 October 1949 in England, and the following year in the United States (Boston: Houghton Mifflin). Allen & Unwin marketed it as a children's book, as they had *The Hobbit* twelve years earlier, even though

Tolkien had warned as early as July 1938 that *Farmer Giles* had become a story for adults. He also remarked, in July 1947, again referring to the enlarged version made for the Lovelace Society: 'You will note that, whoever may buy it, this story was *not* written *for* children; although as in the case of other books that will not necessarily prevent them from being amused by it' (*Letters*, p. 119). Of course it had been originally for children, and at its heart it was essentially unchanged from its earliest versions. Even in its published form it recalls 'The Reluctant Dragon' by Kenneth Grahame and the several dragon stories by E. Nesbit. But Tolkien intended his later, more sophisticated text to be read, or heard told, mainly by an older public who could better appreciate its subtleties. In fact it was already being so read, circulated by Tolkien in typescript to friends such as his Oxford student, the future storyteller Roger Lancelyn Green.

Farmer Giles of Ham did not become a classic of children's literature like *The Hobbit*. However, it has appealed to readers of all ages for half a century. It is a lively story, told with intelligence and wit. Also it is interesting as one of the few works of fiction by Tolkien that is wholly distinct from the 'matter of Middle-earth' – he kept it apart from his invented mythology 'with an effort' (*Letters*, p. 136). Nevertheless there are a few points of similarity between the present story and Tolkien's more famous writings, the most obvious of which is that Giles, like Bilbo the hobbit, is a reluctant and unlikely hero drawn out of a comfortable life into unexpected adventures.

For this new printing of *Farmer Giles of Ham* the original edition of 1949 has been reproduced in facsimile. By this method the text and illustrations have been restored to the setting that Pauline Baynes carefully devised in concert with Allen & Unwin, and Tolkien approved. At the end of the volume we have added a section of notes (by no means exhaustive) about Tolkien's literary and historical sources for *Farmer Giles*, uncommon words and phrases, and other points that seem to us of special interest. These are keyed to page numbers, without superscript references in the text, so that those who prefer to read the story and ancillary material without the interruption of apparatus may do so.

Following the text proper, and published for the first time, are the earliest written (manuscript) version of *Farmer Giles,* and Tolkien's abandoned sequel. In transcribing the former we altered, for consistency, only a few marks of punctuation and a few instances of capitalization. But the latter, four pages of draft passages and notes preserved in the Bodleian Library, written in a difficult script with many starts and stops, needed more serious editing for ease of reading.

The first version of *Farmer Giles of Ham*, as we have said, was shorter and less sophisticated than the published book. It is very interesting, however, as *Roverandom* is interesting, as an example of a story in the form that Tolkien told it to his children, or as close to its original form as one can now approach. It also provides a useful comparison to the final text, with which to measure the progress of a story from invention to publication.

The unfinished sequel to *Farmer Giles* likewise sheds light on the process of storytelling, and of course is inherently interesting for its elements of plot and character. The manuscript is regrettably brief. Even in so preliminary a form it promises a story as lively as *Farmer Giles* and as rich in humour and allusion. Tolkien thought at first to set the new tale at a time after Giles had died and his son George had succeeded to the throne of the Little Kingdom. After a few sentences he changed his mind, perhaps because he could not think of an interesting story to tell about *King* George; however, he immediately began a new approach, with Giles still alive and the story concerned with *Prince* George as he changed from a rustic lad into a worthy monarch. It is a very rough beginning, written quickly with a great deal of emendation, though it forms a coherent narrative. Unfortunately it breaks off, in mid-sentence, after only two manuscript pages, but is followed by a two-page outline of the rest of the story.

On 24 July 1938 Tolkien referred in a letter to Allen & Unwin to 'two or three other stories', not yet written, which were then wanted by the publisher to accompany *Farmer Giles of Ham* (*Letters*, p. 39). On 31 August 1938 he wrote again, that he had 'planned out a sequel' (*Letters*, p. 40). It is possible that such work as was done on the one sequel for which notes exist took place between these two letters. In later correspondence Tolkien continued to refer to more stories in this vein, as well as to the sequel plotted but incomplete, 'the adventures of Prince George (the farmer's son) and the fat boy Suovetaurilius (vulgarly Suet), and the Battle of Otmoor' (10 February 1939, *Letters*, p. 43). Once Allen & Unwin decided to publish *Farmer Giles* with no accompanying stories, the plotted sequel was set aside, though not forgotten. Tolkien slyly alludes to it in the published foreword (p. 8) as if it were a real artifact, a fragment from ancient days. In truth it remained no more than a fragment, as Tolkien found it impossible to recapture the spirit that had inspired his original tale of the Little Kingdom.

For their aid and advice in the making of this book we would like to thank John, Priscilla, Joanna, and especially Christopher Tolkien; Charles B. Elston, Archivist of Marquette University, and his staff; Colin Harris of the Department of Western Manuscripts, Bodleian Library; Joanna Parker, Librarian of Worcester College, Oxford; the staff of the Williams College Library, Williamstown, Massachusetts; David Brawn and Chris Smith of HarperCollins; Pauline Baynes; Charles Fuqua; Carl Hostetter; Rayner Unwin; and Johan Vanhecke. We are also grateful to those authors whose writings on *Farmer Giles of Ham* we have found helpful, in particular Jane Chance, David Doughan, Brin Dunsire, Paul H. Kocher, Dylan Pugh, John D. Rateliff, the late Taum Santoski, and Tom Shippey.

Christina Scull
Wayne G. Hammond

FOREWORD

OF the history of the Little Kingdom few fragments
have survived; but by chance an account of its origin
has been preserved: a legend, perhaps, rather than
an account; for it is evidently a late compilation, full
of marvels, derived not from sober annals, but from
the popular lays to which its author frequently refers.
For him the events that he records lay already in a
distant past; but he seems, nonetheless, to have lived
himself in the lands of the Little Kingdom. Such
geographical knowledge as he shows (it is not his
strong point) is of that country, while of regions
outside it, north or west, he is plainly ignorant.

An excuse for presenting a translation of this
curious tale, out of its very insular Latin into the
modern tongue of the United Kingdom, may be
found in the glimpse that it affords of life in a dark
period of the history of Britain, not to mention the
light that it throws on the origin of some difficult
place-names. Some may find the character and adventures of its hero attractive in themselves.

The boundaries of the Little Kingdom, either in
time or space, are not easy to determine from the
scanty evidence. Since Brutus came to Britain many
kings and realms have come and gone. The partition
under Locrin, Camber, and Albanac, was only the
first of many shifting divisions. What with the love
of petty independence on the one hand, and on the
other the greed of kings for wider realms, the years
were filled with swift alternations of war and peace,
of mirth and woe, as historians of the reign of Arthur
tell us: a time of unsettled frontiers, when men might

7

rise or fall suddenly, and songwriters had abundant material and eager audiences. Somewhere in those long years, after the days of King Coel maybe, but before Arthur or the Seven Kingdoms of the English, we must place the events here related; and their scene is the valley of the Thames, with an excursion north-west to the walls of Wales.

The capital of the Little Kingdom was evidently, as is ours, in its south-east corner, but its confines are vague. It seems never to have reached far up the Thames into the West, nor beyond Otmoor to the North; its eastern borders are dubious. There are indications in a fragmentary legend of Georgius son of Giles and his page Suovetaurilius (Suet) that at one time an outpost against the Middle Kingdom was maintained at Farthingho. But that situation does not concern this story, which is now presented without alteration or further comment, though the original grandiose title has been suitably reduced to *Farmer Giles of Ham.*

FARMER GILES OF HAM

ÆGIDIUS DE HAMMO was a man who lived in the midmost parts of the Island of Britain. In full his name was Ægidius Ahenobarbus Julius Agricola de Hammo; for people were richly endowed with names in those days, now long ago, when this island was still happily divided into many kingdoms: There was more time then, and folk were fewer, so that most men were distinguished. However, those days are now over, so I will in what follows give the man his name shortly, and in the vulgar form: he was Farmer Giles of Ham, and he had a red beard. Ham was only a village, but villages were proud and independent still in those days.

Farmer Giles had a dog. The dog's name was Garm. Dogs had to be content with short names·in the vernacular: the Book-latin was reserved for their betters. Garm could not talk even dog-latin; but he could use the vulgar tongue (as could most dogs of his day) either to bully or to brag or to wheedle in. Bullying was for beggars and trespassers, bragging

9

for other dogs, and wheedling for his master. Garm was both proud and afraid of Giles, who could bully and brag better than he could.

The time was not one of hurry or bustle. But bustle has very little to do with business. Men did their work without it; and they got through a deal both of work and of talk. There was plenty to talk about, for memorable events occurred very frequently. But at the moment when this tale begins nothing memorable had, in fact, happened in Ham for quite a long time. Which suited Farmer Giles down to the ground: he was a slow sort of fellow, rather set in his ways, and taken up with his own affairs. He had his hands full (he said) keeping the wolf from the door: that is, keeping himself as fat and comfortable as his father before him. The dog was busy helping him. Neither of them gave much thought to the Wide World outside their fields, the village, and the nearest market.

But the Wide World was there. The forest was not far off, and away west and north were the Wild Hills, and the dubious marches of the mountain-country. And among other things still at large there were giants: rude and uncultured folk, and troublesome at times. There was one giant in particular, larger and more stupid than his fellows. I find no mention of his name in the histories, but it does not matter. He was very

large, his walking-stick was like a tree, and his tread
was heavy. He brushed elms aside like tall grasses;
and he was the ruin of roads and the desolation of
gardens, for his great feet made holes in them as deep
as wells; if he stumbled into a house, that was the
end of it. And all this damage he did wherever he
went, for his head was far above the roofs of houses
and left his feet to look after themselves. He was
near-sighted and
also rather deaf.
Fortunately he
lived far off in
the Wild, and
seldom visited
the lands inhabi-
ted by men, at
least not on pur-
pose. He had a
great tumble-
down house

away up in the mountains; but he had very few
friends, owing to his deafness and his stupidity, and
the scarcity of giants. He used to go out walking in
the Wild Hills and in the empty regions at the feet of
the mountains, all by himself.

One fine summer's day this giant went out for a
walk, and wandered aimlessly along, doing a great
deal of damage in the woods. Suddenly he noticed
that the sun was setting, and felt that his supper-
time was drawing near; but he discovered that he
was in a part of the country that he did not know at
all and had lost his way. Making a wrong guess at

the right direction he walked and he walked until it was dark night. Then he sat down and waited for the moon to rise. Then he walked and walked in the moonlight, striding out with a will, for he was anxious to get home. He had left his best copper pot on the fire, and feared that the bottom would be burned. But his back was to the mountains, and he was already in the lands inhabited by men. He was, indeed, now drawing near to the farm of Ægidius Ahenobarbus Julius Agricola and the village called (in the vulgar tongue) Ham.

It was a fine night. The cows were in the fields, and Farmer Giles's dog had got out and gone for a walk on his own account. He had a fancy for moonshine, and rabbits. He had no idea, of course, that a giant was also out for a walk. That would have given him a good reason for going out without leave, but a still better reason for staying quiet in the kitchen. At about two o'clock the giant arrived in Farmer Giles's fields, broke the hedges, trampled on the crops, and flattened the mowing-grass. In five minutes he had done more damage than the royal fox-hunt could have done in five days.

Garm heard a thump-thump coming along the river-bank, and he ran to the west side of the low hill on which the farmhouse stood, just to see what was happening. Suddenly he saw the giant stride right across the river and tread upon Galathea, the farmer's favourite cow, squashing the poor beast as flat as the farmer could have squashed a blackbeetle.

That was more than enough for Garm. He gave a yelp of fright and bolted home. Quite forgetting that he was out without leave, he came and barked and yammered underneath his master's bedroom window.

There was no answer for a long time. Farmer Giles was not easily wakened. "Help! help! help!" cried Garm. The window opened suddenly and a well-aimed bottle came flying out.

"Ow!" said the dog, jumping aside with practised skill. "Help! help! help!"

Out popped the farmer's head. "Drat you, dog! What be you a-doing?" said he.

"Nothing," said the dog.

"I'll give you nothing! I'll flay the skin off you in the morning," said the farmer, slamming the window.

"Help! help! help!" cried the dog.

Out came Giles's head again. "I'll kill you, if you make another sound," he said. "What's come to you, you fool?"

"Nothing," said the dog; "but something's come to you."

"What d'you mean?" said Giles, startled in the midst of his rage. Never before had Garm answered him saucily.

"There's a giant in your fields, an enormous giant;

13

and he's coming this way," said the dog. "Help! help! He is trampling on your sheep. He has stamped on poor Galathea, and she's as flat as a doormat. Help! help! He's bursting all your hedges, and he's crushing all your crops. You must be bold and quick, master, or you will soon have nothing left. Help!" Garm began to howl.

"Shut up!" said the farmer, and he shut the window. "Lord-a-mercy!" he said to himself; and though the night was warm, he shivered and shook.

"Get back to bed and don't be a fool!" said his wife. "And drown that dog in the morning. There is no call to believe what a dog says: they'll tell any tale, when caught truant or thieving."

"May be, Agatha," said he, "and may be not. But there's something going on in my fields, or Garm's a rabbit. That dog was frightened. And why should he come yammering in the night when he could sneak in at the back door with the milk in the morning?"

"Don't stand there arguing!" said she. "If you believe the dog, then take his advice: be bold and quick!"

"Easier said than done," answered Giles; for, indeed, he believed quite half of Garm's tale. In the small hours of the night giants seem less unlikely.

Still, property is property; and Farmer Giles had a short way with trespassers that few could outface. So he pulled on his breeches, and went down into the kitchen and took his blunderbuss from the wall. Some may well ask what a blunderbuss was. Indeed, this very question, it is said, was put to the Four Wise Clerks of Oxenford, and after thought they replied: "A blunderbuss is a short gun with a large bore firing many balls or slugs, and capable of doing execution within a limited range without exact aim. (Now superseded in civilized countries by other firearms.)"

However, Farmer Giles's blunderbuss had a wide mouth that opened like a horn, and it did not fire balls or slugs, but anything that he could spare to stuff in. And it did not do execution, because he seldom loaded it, and never let it off. The sight of it was usually enough for his purpose. And this country was not yet civilized, for the blunderbuss was not superseded: it was indeed the only kind of gun that there was, and rare at that. People preferred bows and arrows and used gunpowder mostly for fireworks.

Well then, Farmer Giles took down the blunderbuss, and he put in a good charge of powder, just in case extreme measures should be required; and into the wide mouth he stuffed old nails and bits of wire, pieces of broken pot, bones and stones and other rubbish. Then he drew on his top-boots and his overcoat, and he went out through the kitchen garden.

The moon was low behind him, and he could see nothing worse than the long black shadows of

15

bushes and trees; but he could hear a dreadful stamping-stumping coming up the side of the hill. He did not feel either bold or quick, whatever Agatha might say; but he was more anxious about his property than his skin. So, feeling a bit loose about the belt, he walked towards the brow of the hill.

Suddenly up over the edge of it the giant's face appeared, pale in the moonlight, which glittered in his large round eyes. His feet were still far below, making holes in the fields. The moon dazzled the giant and he did not see the farmer; but Farmer Giles saw him and was scared out of his wits. He pulled the trigger without thinking, and the blunder-buss went off with a staggering bang. By luck it was pointed more or less at the giant's large ugly face. Out flew the rubbish, and the stones and the bones, and the bits of crock and wire, and half a dozen nails. And since the range was indeed limited, by chance and no choice of the farmer's many of these things struck the giant: a piece of pot went in his eye, and a large nail stuck in his nose.

"Blast!" said the giant in his vulgar fashion. "I'm stung!" The noise had made no impression on him (he was rather deaf), but he did not like the nail. It was a long time since he had met any insect fierce enough to pierce his thick skin; but he had heard tell that away East, in the Fens, there were dragon-flies that could bite like hot pincers. He thought that he must have run into something of the kind.

"Nasty unhealthy parts, evidently," said he. "I shan't go any further this way tonight."

So he picked up a couple of sheep off the hill-side, to eat when he got home, and went back over the river, making off about nor-nor-west at a great pace. He found his way home again in the end, for he was at last going in the right direction; but the bottom was burned off his copper pot.

As for Farmer Giles, when the blunderbuss went off it knocked him over flat on his back; and there he lay looking at the sky and wondering if the giant's feet would miss him as they passed by. But nothing happened, and the stamping-stumping died away in the distance. So he got up, rubbed his shoulder, and picked up the blunderbuss. Then suddenly he heard the sound of people cheering.

Most of the people of Ham had been looking out of their windows; a few had put on their clothes and come out (after the giant had gone away). Some were now running up the hill shouting.

The villagers had heard the horrible thump-thump of the giant's feet, and most of them had immediately got under the bed-clothes; some had got under the beds. But Garm was both proud and frightened of his master. He thought him terrible and splendid, when he was angry; and he naturally thought that any giant would think the same. So, as soon as he saw Giles come out with the blunderbuss (a sign of great wrath as a rule), he rushed off to the village, barking and crying:

"Come out! Come out! Come out! Get up! Get up! Come and see my great master! He is bold and quick. He is going to shoot a giant for trespassing. Come out!"

The top of the hill could be seen from most of the houses. When the people and the dog saw the giant's face rise above it, they quailed and held their breath, and all but the dog among them thought that this would prove a matter too big for Giles to deal with. Then the blunderbuss went bang, and the giant turned suddenly and went away, and in their amazement and their joy they clapped and cheered, and Garm nearly barked his head off.

"Hooray!" they shouted. "That will learn him! Master Ægidius has given him what for. Now he will go home and die, and serve him right and proper." Then they all cheered again together. But even as they cheered, they took note for their own profit that after all this blunderbuss could really be fired. There had been some debate in the village inns on that point; but now the matter was settled. Farmer Giles had little trouble with trespassers after that.

When all seemed safe some of the bolder folk came right up the hill and shook hands with Farmer Giles. A few—the parson, and the blacksmith, and the miller, and one or two other persons of importance—slapped him on the back. That did not please him (his shoulder was very sore), but he felt obliged to invite them into his house. They sat round in the

18

kitchen drinking his health and loudly praising him. He made no effort to hide his yawns, but as long as the drink lasted they took no notice. By the time they had all had one or two (and the farmer two or three), he began to feel quite bold; when they had all had two or three (and he himself five or six), he felt as bold as his dog thought him. They parted good friends; and he slapped their backs heartily. His hands were large, red, and thick; so he had his revenge.

Next day he found that the news had grown in the telling, and he had become an important local figure. By the middle of the next week the news had spread to all the villages within twenty miles. He had become the Hero of the Countryside. Very pleasant he found it. Next market day he got enough free drink to float a boat: that is to say, he nearly had his fill, and came home singing old heroic songs.

At last even the King got to hear of it. The capital of that realm, the Middle Kingdom of the island in those happy days, was some twenty leagues distant from Ham, and they paid little heed at court, as a rule, to the doings of rustics in the provinces. But so

prompt an expulsion of a giant so injurious seemed worthy of note and of some little courtesy. So in due course—that is, in about three months, and on the feast of St. Michael—the King sent a magnificent letter. It was written in red upon white parchment, and expressed the royal approbation of "our loyal subject and well-beloved Ægidius Ahenobarbus Julius Agricola de Hammo."

The letter was signed with a red blot; but the court scribe had added: 𝕰𝖌𝖔 𝕬𝖚𝖌𝖚𝖘𝖙𝖚𝖘 𝕭𝖔𝖓𝖎𝖋𝖆𝖈𝖎𝖚𝖘 𝕬𝖒𝖇𝖗𝖔𝖘𝖎𝖚𝖘 𝕬𝖚𝖗𝖊𝖑𝖎𝖆𝖓𝖚𝖘 𝕬𝖓𝖙𝖔𝖓𝖎𝖓𝖚𝖘 𝕻𝖎𝖚𝖘 𝖊𝖙 𝕸𝖆𝖌𝖓𝖎𝖋𝖎𝖈𝖚𝖘, 𝖉𝖚𝖝, 𝖗𝖊𝖝, 𝖙𝖞𝖗𝖆𝖓𝖓𝖚𝖘, 𝖊𝖙 𝕭𝖆𝖘𝖎𝖑𝖊𝖚𝖘 𝕸𝖊𝖉𝖎𝖙𝖊𝖗𝖗𝖆𝖓𝖊𝖆𝖗𝖚𝖒 𝕻𝖆𝖗𝖙𝖎𝖚𝖒, 𝖘𝖚𝖇𝖘𝖈𝖗𝖎𝖇𝖔; and a large red seal was attached. So the document was plainly genuine. It afforded great pleasure to Giles, and was much admired, especially when it was discovered that one could get a seat and a drink by the farmer's fire by asking to look at it.

Better than the testimonial was the accompanying gift. The King sent a belt and a long sword. To tell

the truth the King had never used the sword himself. It belonged to the family and had been hanging in his armoury time out of mind. The armourer could not say how it came there, or what might be the use of it. Plain heavy swords of that kind were out of fashion at court just then, so the King thought it the very thing for a present to a rustic. But Farmer Giles was delighted, and his local reputation became enormous.

Giles much enjoyed the turn of events. So did his dog. He never got his promised whipping. Giles was a just man according to his lights; in his heart he gave a fair share of the credit to Garm, though he never went so far as to mention it. He continued to

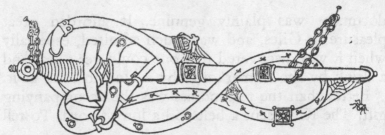

throw hard words and hard things at the dog when he felt inclined, but he winked at many little outings. Garm took to walking far afield. The farmer went about with a high step, and luck smiled on him. The autumn and early winter work went well. All seemed set fair—until the dragon came.

In those days dragons were already getting scarce in the island. None had been seen in the midland realm of Augustus Bonifacius for many a year. There were, of course, the dubious marches and the uninhabited mountains, westward and northward, but they were a long way off. In those parts once upon a time there had dwelt a number of dragons of one kind and another, and they had made raids far and wide. But the Middle Kingdom was in those days famous for the daring of the King's knights, and so many stray dragons had been killed, or had returned with grave damage, that the others gave up going that way.

It was still the custom for Dragon's Tail to be served up at the King's Christmas Feast; and each year a knight was chosen for the duty of hunting. He was supposed to set out upon St. Nicholas' Day and come home with a dragon's tail not later than the eve of the feast. But for many years now the Royal Cook had made a marvellous confection, a Mock Dragon's

22

Tail of cake and almond-paste, with cunning scales of hard icing-sugar. The chosen knight then carried this into the hall on Christmas Eve, while the fiddles played and the trumpets rang. The Mock Dragon's Tail was eaten after dinner on Christmas Day, and everybody said (to please the cook) that it tasted much better than Real Tail.

That was the situation when a real dragon turned up again. The giant was largely to blame. After his adventure he used to go about in the mountains visiting his scattered relations more than had been his custom, and much more than they liked. For he was always trying to borrow a large copper pot. But whether he got the loan of one or not, he would sit and talk in his long-winded lumbering fashion about the excellent country down away East, and all the wonders of the Wide World. He had got it into his head that he was a great and daring traveller.

"A nice land," he would say, "pretty flat, soft to the feet, and plenty to eat for the taking: cows, you know, and sheep all over the place, easy to spot, if you look carefully."

"But what about the people?" said they.

"I never saw any," said he. "There was not a knight to be seen or heard, my dear fellows. Nothing worse than a few stinging flies by the river."

"Why don't you go back and stay there?" said they.

"Oh well, there's no place like home, they say," said he. "But maybe I shall go back one day when I have a mind. And anyway I went there once, which is more than most folk can say. Now about that copper pot."

"And these rich lands," they would hurriedly ask, "these delectable regions full of undefended cattle, which way do they lie? And how far off?"

"Oh," he would answer, "away east or sou'east. But it's a long journey." And then he would give such an exaggerated account of the distance that he had walked, and the woods, hills, and plains that he had crossed, that none of the other less long-legged giants ever set out. Still, the talk got about.

Then the warm summer was followed by a hard winter. It was bitter cold in the mountains and food

was scarce. The talk got louder. Lowland sheep and kine from the deep pastures were much discussed. The dragons pricked up their ears. They were

24

hungry, and these rumours were attractive.

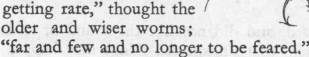

"So knights are mythical!" said the younger and less experienced dragons. "We always thought so."

"At least they may be getting rare," thought the older and wiser worms; "far and few and no longer to be feared."

There was one dragon who was deeply moved. Chrysophylax Dives was his name, for he was of ancient and imperial lineage, and very rich. He was cunning, inquisitive, greedy, well-armoured, but not over bold. But at any rate he was not in the least afraid of flies or insects of any sort or size; and he was mortally hungry.

So one winter's day, about a week before Christmas, Chrysophylax spread his wings and took off. He landed quietly in the middle of the night plump in the heart of the midland realm of Augustus Bonifacius rex et basileus. He did a deal of damage in a short while, smashing and burning, and devouring sheep, cattle, and horses.

This was in a part of the land a long way from Ham, but Garm got the fright of his life. He had gone off on a long expedition, and taking advantage of his master's favour he had ventured to spend a night or two away from home. He was following an engaging scent along the eaves of a wood, when he turned a corner and came suddenly upon a new and alarming smell; he ran indeed slap into the tail of

Chrysophylax Dives, who had just landed. Never did a dog turn his own tail round and bolt home swifter than Garm. The dragon, hearing his yelp, turned and snorted; but Garm was already far out of range. He ran all the rest of the night, and arrived home about breakfast-time.

"Help! help! help!" he cried outside the back door.

Giles heard, and did not like the sound of it. It reminded him that unexpected things may happen, when all seems to be going well.

"Wife, let that dratted dog in," said he, "and take a stick to him!"

Garm came bundling into the kitchen with his eyes starting and his tongue hanging out. "Help!" he cried.

"Now what have you been a-doing this time?" said Giles, throwing a sausage at him.

"Nothing," panted Garm, too flustered to give heed to the sausage.

"Well, stop doing it, or I'll skin you," said the farmer.

26

"I've done no wrong. I didn't mean no harm," said the dog. "But I came on a dragon accidental-like, and it frightened me."

The farmer choked in his beer. "Dragon?" said he. "Drat you for a good-for-nothing nosey-parker! What d'you want to go and find a dragon for, at this time of the year, and me with my hands full? Where was it?"

"Oh! North over the hills and far away, beyond the Standing Stones and all," said the dog.

"Oh, away there!" said Giles, mighty relieved. "They're queer folk in those parts, I've heard tell, and aught might happen in their land. Let them get on with it! Don't come worriting me with such tales. Get out!"

Garm got out, and spread the news all over the village. He did not forget to mention that his master was not scared in the least. "Quite cool he was, and went on with his breakfast."

People chatted about it pleasantly at their doors. "How like old times!" they said. "Just as Christmas is coming, too. So seasonable. How pleased the King will be! He will be able to have Real Tail this Christmas."

But more news came in next day. The dragon, it appeared, was exceptionally large and ferocious. He was doing terrible damage.

"What about the King's knights?" people began to say.

Others had already asked the same question. Indeed, messengers were now reaching the King from the villages most afflicted by Chrysophylax, and they said to him as loudly and as often as they dared: "Lord, what of your knights?"

But the knights did nothing; their knowledge of the dragon was still quite unofficial. So the King brought the matter to their notice, fully and formally, asking for necessary action at their early convenience. He was greatly displeased when he found that their convenience would not be early at all, and was indeed daily postponed.

Yet the excuses of the knights were undoubtedly sound. First of all, the Royal Cook had already made the Dragon's Tail for that Christmas, being a man who believed in getting things done in good time. It would not do at all to offend him by bringing in a real tail at the last minute. He was a very valuable servant.

"Never mind the Tail! Cut his head off and put an end to him!" cried the messengers from the villages most nearly affected.

But Christmas had arrived, and most unfortunately a grand tournament had been arranged for St. John's Day: knights of many realms had been invited and were coming to compete for a valuable prize. It was obviously unreasonable to spoil the chances of the Midland Knights by sending their best men off on a dragon-hunt before the tournament was over.

After that came the New Year Holiday.

But each night the dragon had moved; and each move had brought him nearer to Ham. On the night of New Year's Day people could see a blaze in the distance. The dragon had settled in a wood about ten miles away, and it was burning merrily. He was a hot dragon when he felt in the mood.

28

After that people began to look at Farmer Giles and whisper behind his back. It made him very uncomfortable; but he pretended not to notice it. The next day the dragon came several miles nearer. Then Farmer Giles himself began to talk loudly of the scandal of the King's knights.

"I should like to know what they do to earn their keep," said he.

"So should we!" said everyone in Ham.

But the miller added: "Some men still get knighthood by sheer merit, I am told. After all, our good Ægidius here is already a knight in a manner of speaking. Did not the King send him a red letter and a sword?"

"There's more to knighthood than a sword," said Giles. "There's dubbing and all that, or so I understand. Anyway I've my own business to attend to."

"Oh! but the King would do the dubbing, I don't doubt, if he were asked," said the miller. "Let us ask him, before it is too late!"

"Nay!" said Giles. "Dubbing is not for my sort.

I am a farmer and proud of it: a plain honest man, and honest men fare ill at court, they say. It is more in your line, Master Miller."

The parson smiled: not at the farmer's retort, for Giles and the miller were always giving one another as good as they got, being bosom enemies, as the saying was in Ham. The parson had suddenly been struck with a notion that pleased him, but he said no more at that time. The miller was not so pleased, and he scowled.

"Plain certainly, and honest perhaps," said he. "But do you have to go to court and be a knight before you kill a dragon? Courage is all that is needed, as only yesterday I heard Master Ægidius declare. Surely he has as much courage as any knight?"

All the folk standing by shouted: "Of course not!" and "Yes indeed! Three cheers for the Hero of Ham!"

Then Farmer Giles went home feeling very uncomfortable. He was finding that a local reputation may require keeping up, and that may prove awkward. He kicked the dog, and hid the sword in a cupboard in the kitchen. Up till then it had hung over the fireplace.

The next day the dragon moved to the neighbouring village of Quercetum (Oakley in the vulgar tongue). He ate not only sheep and cows and one or two persons of tender age, but he ate the parson too. Rather rashly the parson had sought to dissuade him from his evil ways. Then there was a terrible commotion. All the people of Ham came up the hill, headed by their own parson; and they waited on Farmer Giles.

"We look to you!" they said; and they remained standing round and looking, until the farmer's face was redder than his beard.

"When are you going to start?" they asked.

"Well, I can't start today, and that's a fact," said he. "I've a lot on hand with my cowman sick and all. I'll see about it."

They went away; but in the evening it was rumoured that the dragon had moved even nearer, so they all came back.

"We look to you, Master Ægidius," they said.

"Well," said he, "it's very awkward for me just now. My mare has gone lame, and the lambing has started. I'll see about it as soon as may be."

So they went away once more, not without some grumbling and whispering. The miller was sniggering. The parson stayed behind, and could not be got rid of. He invited himself to supper, and made some pointed remarks. He even asked what had become of the sword and insisted on seeing it.

It was lying in a cupboard on a shelf hardly long enough for it, and as soon as Farmer Giles brought it out in a flash it leaped from the sheath, which the farmer dropped as if it had been hot. The parson sprang to his feet, upsetting his beer. He picked the sword up carefully and tried to put it back in the sheath; but it would not go so much as a foot in, and it jumped clean out again, as soon as he took his hand off the hilt.

"Dear me! This is very peculiar!" said the parson, and he took a good look at both scabbard and blade. He was a lettered man, but the farmer could only spell out large uncials with difficulty, and was none too sure of the reading even of his own name. That is why he had never given any heed to the strange letters that could dimly be seen on sheath and sword. As for the King's armourer, he was so accustomed to runes, names, and other signs of power and significance upon swords and scabbards that he had not bothered his head about them; he thought them out of date, anyway.

But the parson looked long, and he frowned. He had expected to find some lettering on the sword or on the scabbard, and that was indeed the idea that had come to him the day before; but now he was surprised at what he saw, for letters and signs there were, to be sure, but he could not make head or tail of them.

"There is an inscription on this sheath, and some, ah, epigraphical signs are visible also upon the sword," he said.

"Indeed?" said Giles. "And what may that amount to?"

"The characters are archaic and the language barbaric," said the parson, to gain time. "A little closer inspection will be required." He begged the loan of the sword for the night, and the farmer let him have it with pleasure.

When the parson got home he took down many

learned books from his shelves, and he sat up far into the night. Next morning it was discovered that the dragon had moved nearer still. All the people of Ham barred their doors and shuttered their windows; and those that had cellars went down into them and sat shivering in the candle-light.

But the parson stole out and went from door to door; and he told, to all who would listen through a crack or a keyhole, what he had discovered in his study.

"Our good Ægidius," he said, "by the King's grace is now the owner of Caudimordax, the famous sword that in popular romances is more vulgarly called Tailbiter."

Those that heard this name usually opened the door. They all knew the renown of Tailbiter, for that sword had belonged to Bellomarius, the greatest of all the dragon-slayers of the realm. Some accounts made him the maternal great-great-grandfather of the King. The songs and tales of his deeds were many, and if forgotten at court, were still remembered in the villages.

"This sword," said the parson, "will not stay sheathed, if a dragon is within five miles; and without doubt in a brave man's hands no dragon can resist it."

Then people began to take heart again; and some unshuttered the windows and put their heads out. In the end the parson persuaded a few to come and join him; but only the miller was really willing. To see Giles in a real fix seemed to him worth the risk.

They went up the hill, not without anxious looks north across the river. There was no sign of the dragon. Probably he was asleep; he had been feeding very well all the Christmas-time.

The parson (and the miller) hammered on the farmer's door. There was no answer, so they hammered louder. At last Giles came out. His face was very red. He also had sat up far into the night, drinking a good deal of ale; and he had begun again as soon as he got up.

They all crowded round him, calling him Good Ægidius, Bold Ahenobarbus, Great Julius, Staunch Agricola, Pride of Ham, Hero of the Countryside. And they spoke of Caudimordax, Tailbiter, The Sword that would not be Sheathed, Death or Victory, The Glory of the Yeomanry, Backbone of the Country, and the Good of one's Fellow Men, until the farmer's head was hopelessly confused.

"Now then! One at a time!" he said, when he got a chance. "What's all this, what's all this? It's my busy morning, you know."

So they let the parson explain the situation. Then the miller had the pleasure of seeing the farmer in as tight a fix as he could wish. But things did not turn out quite as the miller expected. For one thing Giles had drunk a deal of strong ale. For another he had a queer feeling of pride and encouragement when he learned that his sword was actually Tailbiter. He had been very fond of tales about Bellomarius when he was a boy, and before he had learned sense he had sometimes wished that he could have a marvellous and heroic sword of his own. So it came over him all of a sudden that he would take Tailbiter and go dragon-hunting. But he had been used to bargaining all his life, and he made one more effort to postpone the event.

"What!" said he. "Me go dragon-hunting? In my old leggings and waistcoat? Dragon-fights need some kind of armour, from all I've heard tell. There isn't any armour in this house, and that's a fact," said he.

That was a bit awkward, they all allowed; but they sent for the blacksmith. The blacksmith shook his head. He was a slow, gloomy man, vulgarly known as Sunny Sam, though his proper name was Fabricius Cunctator. He never whistled at his work, unless some disaster (such as frost in May) had duly occurred after he had foretold it. Since he was daily foretelling disasters of every kind, few happened that he had not foretold, and he was able to take the credit of them. It was his chief pleasure; so naturally he was reluctant to do anything to avert them. He shook his head again.

"I can't make armour out of naught," he said. "And it's not in my line. You'd best get the carpenter to make you a wooden shield. Not that it will help you much. He's a hot dragon."

Their faces fell; but the miller was not so easily to be turned from his plan of sending Giles to the dragon, if he would go; or of blowing the bubble of his local reputation, if he refused in the end. "What about ring-mail?" he said. "That would be a help; and it need not be very fine. It would be for business and not for showing off at court. What about your old leather jerkin, friend Ægidius? And there is a great pile of links and rings in the smithy. I don't suppose Màster Fabricius himself knows what may be lying there."

"You don't know what you are talking about," said the smith, growing cheerful. "If it's real ring-mail you mean, then you can't have it. It needs the skill of the dwarfs, with every little ring fitting into four others and all. Even if I had the craft, I should be working for weeks. And we shall all be in our graves before them," said he, "or leastways in the dragon."

They all wrung their hands in dismay, and the blacksmith began to smile. But they were now so alarmed that they were unwilling to give up the miller's plan and they turned to him for counsel.

"Well," said he, "I've heard tell that in the old days those that could not buy bright hauberks out of the Southlands would stitch steel rings on a leather shirt and be content with that. Let's see what can be done in that line!"

So Giles had to bring out his old jerkin, and the smith was hurried back to his smithy. There they rummaged in every corner and turned over the pile of old metal, as had not been done for many a year. At the bottom they found, all dull with rust, a whole heap of small rings, fallen from some forgotten coat, such as the miller had spoken of. Sam, more unwilling and gloomy as the task seemed more hopeful, was set to work on the spot, gathering and sorting and cleaning the rings; and when (as he was pleased to point out) these were clearly insufficient for one so broad of back and breast as Master Ægidius, they made him split up old chains and hammer the links into rings as fine as his skill could contrive.

They took the smaller rings of steel and stitched

them on to the breast of the jerkin, and the larger and clumsier rings they stitched on the back; and then, when still more rings were forthcoming, so hard was poor Sam driven, they took a pair of the farmer's breeches and stitched rings on to them. And up on a shelf in a dark nook of the smithy the miller found the old iron frame of a helmet, and he set the cobbler to work, covering it with leather as well as he could.

The work took them all the rest of that day, and all the next day—which was Twelfthnight and the eve of the Epiphany, but festivities were neglected. Farmer Giles celebrated the occasion with more ale than usual; but the dragon mercifully slept. For the moment he had forgotten all about hunger or swords.

Early on the Epiphany they went up the hill,  carrying the strange result of their handiwork. Giles was expecting them. He had now no excuses left to offer; so he put on the mail jerkin and the breeches. The miller sniggered. Then Giles put on his topboots and an old pair of spurs; and also the leather - covered helmet. But at the last moment he clapped an old felt hat over the helmet, and over the mail coat he threw his big grey cloak.

"What is the purpose of that, Master?" they asked.

"Well," said Giles, "if it is your notion to go dragon-hunting jingling and dingling like Canterbury Bells, it ain't mine. It don't seem sense to me to let a dragon know that you are coming along the road sooner than need be. And a helmet's a helmet, and a challenge to battle. Let the worm see only my old hat over the hedge, and maybe I'll get nearer before the trouble begins."

They had stitched on the rings so that they overlapped, each hanging loose over the one below, and jingle they certainly did. The cloak did something to stop the noise of them, but Giles cut a queer figure in his gear. They did not tell him so. They girded the belt round his waist with difficulty, and they hung the scabbard upon it; but he had to carry the sword, for it would no longer stay sheathed, unless held with main strength.

The farmer called for Garm. He was a just man according to his lights. "Dog," he said, "you are coming with me."

The dog howled. "Help! help!" he cried.

"Now stop it!" said Giles. "Or I'll give you worse than any dragon could. You know the smell of this worm, and maybe you'll prove useful for once."

Then Farmer Giles called for his grey mare. She gave him a queer look and sniffed at the spurs. But she let him get up; and then off they went, and none of them felt happy. They trotted through the village, and all the folk clapped and cheered, mostly from their windows. The farmer and his mare put as

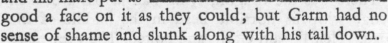

good a face on it as they could; but Garm had no sense of shame and slunk along with his tail down.

They crossed the bridge over the river at the end of the village. When at last they were well out of sight, they slowed to a walk. Yet all too soon they passed out of the lands belonging to Farmer Giles and to other folk of Ham and came to parts that the dragon had visited. There were broken trees, burned hedges and blackened grass, and a nasty uncanny silence.

The sun was shining bright, and Farmer Giles began to wish that he dared shed a garment or two; and he wondered if he had not taken a pint too many. "A nice end to Christmas and all," he thought. "And I'll be lucky if it don't prove the end of me too." He mopped his face with a large handkerchief—green, not red; for red rags infuriate dragons, or so he had heard tell.

But he did not find the dragon. He rode down many lanes, wide and narrow, and over other farmers' deserted fields, and still he did not find the dragon. Garm was, of course, of no use at all. He kept just behind the mare and refused to use his nose.

They came at last to a winding road that had suffered little damage and seemed quiet and peaceful. After following it for half a mile Giles began to wonder whether he had not done his duty and all that his reputation required. He had made up his mind that he had looked long and far enough, and he was just thinking of turning back, and of his dinner, and of telling his friends that the dragon had seen him coming and simply flown away, when he turned a sharp corner.

There was the dragon, lying half across a broken hedge with his horrible head in the middle of the road. "Help!" said Garm and bolted. The grey mare sat down plump, and Farmer Giles went off backwards into a ditch. When he put his head out, there was the dragon wide awake looking at him.

"Good morning!" said the dragon. "You seem surprised."

"Good morning!" said Giles. "I am that."

"Excuse me," said the dragon. He had cocked a very suspicious ear when he caught the sound of rings jingling, as the farmer fell. "Excuse my asking, but were you looking for me, by any chance?"

"No, indeed!" said the farmer. "Who'd a' thought of seeing you here? I was just going for a ride."

He scrambled out of the ditch in a hurry and backed away towards the grey mare. She was now on her feet again and was nibbling some grass at the wayside, seeming quite unconcerned.

"Then we meet by good luck," said the dragon. "The pleasure is mine. Those are your holiday clothes, I suppose. A new fashion, perhaps?" Farmer Giles's felt hat had fallen off and his grey cloak had slipped open; but he brazened it out.

"Aye," said he, "brand-new. But I must be after that dog of mine. He's gone after rabbits, I fancy."

"I fancy not," said Chrysophylax, licking his lips (a sign of amusement). "He will get home a long time before you do, I expect. But pray proceed on your way, Master—let me see, I don't think I know your name?"

"Nor I yours," said Giles; "and we'll leave it at that."

"As you like," said Chrysophylax, licking his lips again, but pretending to close his eyes. He had a wicked heart (as dragons all have), but not a very bold one (as is not unusual). He preferred a meal that he did not have to fight for; but appetite had returned after a good long sleep. The parson of

Oakley had been stringy, and it was years since he had tasted a large fat man. He had now made up his mind to try this easy meat, and he was only waiting until the old fool was off his guard.

But the old fool was not as foolish as he looked, and he kept his eye on the dragon, even while he was trying to mount. The mare, however, had other ideas, and she kicked and shied when Giles tried to get up. The dragon became impatient and made ready to spring.

"Excuse me!" said he. "Haven't you dropped something?"

An ancient trick, but it succeeded; for Giles had indeed dropped something. When he fell he had dropped Caudimordax (or vulgarly Tailbiter), and there it lay by the wayside. He stooped to pick it up; and the dragon sprang. But not as quick as Tailbiter. As soon as it was in the farmer's hand, it leaped forward with a flash, straight at the dragon's eyes.

"Hey!" said the dragon, and stopped very short. "What have you got there?"

"Only Tailbiter, that was given to me by the King," said Giles.

"My mistake!" said the dragon. "I beg your pardon." He lay and grovelled, and Farmer Giles began to feel more comfortable. "I don't think you have treated me fair."

"How not?" said Giles. "And anyway why should I?"

"You have concealed your honourable name and pretended that our meeting was by chance; yet you are plainly a knight of high lineage. It used, sir, to be the custom of knights to issue a challenge in such cases, after a proper exchange of titles and credentials."

"Maybe it used, and maybe it still is," said Giles, beginning to feel pleased with himself. A man who has a large and imperial dragon grovelling before him may be excused, if he feels somewhat uplifted. "But you are making more mistakes than one, old worm. I am no knight. I am Farmer Ægidius of Ham, I am; and I can't abide trespassers. I've shot giants with my blunderbuss before now, for doing less damage than you have. And I issued no challenge neither."

The dragon was disturbed. "Curse that giant for a liar!" he thought. "I have been sadly misled. And now what on earth does one do with a bold farmer and a sword so bright and aggressive?" He could recall no precedent for such a situation. "Chrysophylax is my name," said he, "Chrysophylax the Rich. What can I do for your honour?" he added ingratiatingly, with one eye on the sword, and hoping to escape battle.

"You can take yourself off, you horny old varmint," said Giles, also hoping to escape battle. "I only want to be shut of you. Go right away from here, and get back to your own dirty den!" He stepped towards Chrysophylax, waving his arms as if he was scaring crows.

That was quite enough for Tailbiter. It circled flashing in the air; then down it came, smiting the dragon on the joint of the right wing, a ringing blow that shocked him exceedingly. Of course Giles knew very little about the right methods of killing a dragon, or the sword might have landed in a tenderer spot; but Tailbiter did the best it could in inexperienced hands. It was quite enough for Chrysophylax—he could not use his wing for days. Up he got and turned to fly, and found that he could not. The farmer sprang on the mare's back. The dragon began to run. So did the mare. The dragon galloped over a field puffing and blowing. So did the mare. The farmer bawled and shouted, as if he was watching a horse race; and all the while he waved Tailbiter. The faster the dragon ran the more bewildered he became; and all the while the grey mare put her best leg foremost and kept close behind him.

On they pounded down the lanes, and through the gaps in the fences, over many fields and across many brooks. The dragon was smoking and bellowing and

44

losing all sense of direction. At last they came suddenly to the bridge of Ham, thundered over it, and came roaring down the village street. There Garm had the impudence to sneak out of an alley and join in the chase.

All the people were at their windows or on the roofs. Some laughed and some cheered; and some beat tins and pans and kettles; and others blew horns and pipes and whistles; and the parson had the church bells rung. Such a to-do and an on-going had not been heard in Ham for a hundred years.

Just outside the church the dragon gave up. He lay down in the middle of the road and gasped. Garm came and sniffed at his tail, but Chrysophylax was past all shame.

"Good people, and gallant warrior," he panted, as Farmer Giles rode up, while the villagers gathered round (at a reasonable distance) with hayforks, poles, and pokers in their hands. "Good people, don't kill me! I am very rich. I will pay for all the damage I have done. I will pay for the funerals of all the people I have killed, especially the parson of Oakley; he shall have a noble cenotaph—though he was rather lean. I will give you each a really good present, if you will only let me go home and fetch it."

"How much?" said the farmer.

"Well," said the dragon, calculating quickly. He noticed that the crowd was rather large. "Thirteen and eightpence each?"

"Nonsense!" said Giles. "Rubbish!" said the people. "Rot!" said the dog.

"Two golden guineas each, and children half price?" said the dragon.

"What about dogs?" said Garm. "Go on!" said the farmer. "We're listening."

"Ten pounds and a purse of silver for every soul, and gold collars for the dogs?" said Chrysophylax anxiously.

"Kill him!" shouted the people, getting impatient.

"A bag of gold for everybody, and diamonds for the ladies?" said Chrysophylax hurriedly.

"Now you talking, but not good enough," said Farmer Giles. "You've left dogs out again," said

Garm. "What size of bags?" said the men. "How many diamonds?" said their wives.

"Dear me! dear me!" said the dragon. "I shall be ruined."

"You deserve it," said Giles. "You can choose between being ruined and being killed where you lie." He brandished Tailbiter, and the dragon cowered.

46

"Make up your mind!" the people cried, getting bolder and drawing nearer.

Chrysophylax blinked; but deep down inside him he laughed: a silent quiver which they did not observe. Their bargaining had begun to amuse him. Evidently they expected to get something out of it. They knew very little of the ways of the wide and wicked world —indeed, there was no one now living in all the realm who had had any actual experience in dealing with dragons and their tricks. Chrysophylax was getting his breath back, and his wits as well. He licked his lips.

"Name your own price!" he said.

Then they all began to talk at once. Chrysophylax listened with interest. Only one voice disturbed him: that of the blacksmith.

"No good 'll come of it, mark my words," said he. "A worm won't return, say what you like. But no good will come of it, either way."

"You can stand out of the bargain, if that's your mind," they said to him, and went on haggling, taking little further notice of the dragon.

Chrysophylax raised his head; but if he thought of springing on them, or of slipping off during the argument, he was disappointed. Farmer Giles was standing by, chewing a straw and considering; but Tailbiter was in his hand, and his eye was on the dragon.

"You lie where you be!" said he, "or you'll get what you deserve, gold or no gold."

The dragon lay flat. At last the parson was made spokesman and he stepped up beside Giles. "Vile Worm!" he said. "You must bring back to this spot all your ill-gotten wealth; and after recompensing

47

those whom you have injured we will share it fairly among ourselves. Then, if you make a solemn vow never to disturb our land again, nor to stir up any other monster to trouble us, we will let you depart with both your head and your tail to your own home. And now you shall take such strong oaths to return (with your ransom) as even the conscience of a worm must hold binding."

Chrysophylax accepted, after a plausible show of hesitation. He even shed hot tears, lamenting his ruin, till there were steaming puddles in the road; but no one was moved by them. He swore many oaths, solemn and astonishing, that he would return with all his wealth on the feast of St. Hilarius and St. Felix. That gave him eight days, and far too short a time for the journey, as even those ignorant of geography might well have reflected. Nonetheless, they let him go, and escorted him as far as the bridge.

"To our next meeting!" he said, as he passed over the river. "I am sure we shall all look forward to it."

"We shall indeed," they said. They were, of course, very foolish. For though the oaths he had taken should have burdened his conscience with sorrow and a great fear of disaster, he had, alas! no conscience at all. And if this regrettable lack in one of imperial lineage was beyond the comprehension of the simple, at the least the parson with his booklearning might have guessed it. Maybe he did. He was a grammarian, and could doubtless see further into the future than others.

The blacksmith shook his head as he went back to his smithy. "Ominous names," he said. "Hilarius and Felix! I don't like the sound of them."

The King, of course, quickly heard the news. It ran through the realm like fire and lost nothing in the telling. The King was deeply moved, for various reasons, not the least being financial; and he made up his mind to ride at once in person to Ham, where such strange things seemed to happen.

He arrived four days after the dragon's departure, coming over the bridge on his white horse, with many knights and trumpeters, and a large baggage-train. All the people had put on their best clothes and lined the street to welcome him. The cavalcade came to a halt in the open space before the church gate. Farmer Giles knelt before the King, when he was presented; but the King told him to rise, and actually patted him on the back. The knights pretended not to observe this familiarity.

The King ordered the whole village to assemble in Farmer Giles's large pasture beside the river; and when they were all gathered together (including Garm, who felt that he was concerned), Augustus Bonifacius rex et basileus was graciously pleased to address them.

He explained carefully that the wealth of the miscreant Chrysophylax all belonged to himself as lord of the land. He passed rather lightly over his claim to be considered suzerain of the mountain-country (which was debatable); but "we make no doubt in any case," said he, "that all the treasure of this worm was stolen from our ancestors. Yet we are, as all know, both just and generous, and our good liege Ægidius shall be suitably rewarded; nor shall any of our loyal subjects in this place go without some token of our esteem, from the parson to the youngest child. For we are well pleased with Ham. Here at least a sturdy and uncorrupted folk still retain the ancient courage of our race." The knights were talking among themselves about the new fashion in hats.

The people bowed and curtsied, and thanked him humbly. But they wished now that they had closed with the dragon's offer of ten pounds all round, and kept the matter private. They knew enough, at any rate, to feel sure that the King's esteem would not rise to that. Garm noticed that there was no mention of dogs. Farmer Giles was the only one of them who was really content. He felt sure of some reward, and was mighty glad anyway to have come safely out of a nasty business with his local reputation higher than ever.

The King did not go away. He pitched his pavilions in Farmer Giles's field, and waited for January the fourteenth, making as merry as he could in a miserable village far from the capital. The royal retinue ate up nearly all the bread, butter, eggs, chickens, bacon and mutton, and drank up every drop of old ale there was in the place in the next three days. Then they began to grumble at short commons. But the King paid handsomely for everything (in tallies to be honoured later by the Exchequer, which he hoped would shortly be richly replenished); so the folk of Ham were well satisfied, not knowing the actual state of the Exchequer.

January the fourteenth came, the feast of Hilarius and of Felix, and everybody was up and about early. The knights put on their armour. The farmer put on his coat of home-made mail, and they smiled openly, until they caught the King's frown. The farmer also put on Tailbiter, and it went into its sheath as easy as butter, and stayed there. The parson looked hard at the sword, and nodded to himself. The blacksmith laughed.

Midday came. People were too anxious to eat much. The afternoon passed slowly. Still Tailbiter showed no sign of leaping from the scabbard. None of the watchers on the hill, nor any of the small boys who had climbed to the tops of tall trees, could see anything by air or by land that might herald the return of the dragon.

The blacksmith walked about whistling; but it was not until evening fell and the stars came out that the other folk of the village began to suspect that the dragon did not mean to come back at all. Still they recalled his many solemn and astonishing oaths and kept on hoping. When, however, midnight struck and the appointed day was over, their disappointment was deep. The blacksmith was delighted.

"I told you so," he said. But they were still not convinced.

"After all he was badly hurt," said some.

"We did not give him enough time," said others. "It is a powerful long way to the mountains, and he would have a lot to carry. Maybe he has had to get help."

But the next day passed and the next. Then they all gave up hope. The King was in a red rage. The victuals and drink had run out, and the knights were grumbling loudly. They wished to go back to the merriments of court. But the King wanted money.

He took leave of his loyal subjects, but he was short and sharp about it; and he cancelled half the tallies on the Exchequer. He was quite cold to Farmer Giles and dismissed him with a nod.

"You will hear from us later," he said, and rode off with his knights and his trumpeters.

The more hopeful and simple-minded thought that a message would soon come from the court to summon Master Ægidius to the King, to be knighted at the least. In a week the message came, but it was of different sort. It was written and signed in triplicate: one copy for Giles; one for the parson; and one to be nailed on the church door. Only the copy addressed to the parson was of any use, for the court-hand was peculiar and as dark to the folk of Ham as the Book-latin. But the parson rendered it into the vulgar tongue and read it from the pulpit. It was short and to the point (for a royal letter); the King was in a hurry.

"We Augustus B. A. A. P and M. rex et cetera make known that we have determined, for the safety of our realm and for the keeping of our honour, that the worm or dragon styling himself Chrysophylax the Rich shall be sought out and condignly punished for his misdemeanours, torts, felonies, and foul perjury. All the knights of our Royal Household are hereby commanded to arm and make ready to ride upon this quest, so soon as Master Ægidius A. J. Agricola shall arrive at this our court. Inasmuch as the said Ægidius has proved himself a trusty man and well able to deal with giants, dragons, and other enemies of the King's peace, now therefore we command him to ride forth at once, and to join the company of our knights with all speed."

People said this was a high honour and next-door to being dubbed. The miller was envious. "Friend Ægidius is rising in the world," said he. "I hope he will know us when he gets back."

"Maybe he never will," said the blacksmith.

"That's enough from you, old horse-face!" said the farmer, mighty put out. "Honour be blowed! If I get back even the miller's company will be welcome. Still, it is some comfort to think that I shall be missing you both for a bit." And with that he left them.

You cannot offer excuses to the King as you can to your neighbours; so lambs or no lambs, ploughing or none, milk or water, he had to get up on his grey mare and go. The parson saw him off.

"I hope you are taking some stout rope with you?" he said.

"What for?" said Giles. "To hang myself?"

"Nay! Take heart, Master Ægidius!" said the parson. "It seems to me that you have a luck that

54

you can trust. But take also a long rope, for you may need it, unless my foresight deceives me. And now farewell, and return safely!"

"Aye! And come back and find all my house and land in a pickle. Blast dragons!" said Giles. Then, stuffing a great coil of rope in a bag by his saddle, he climbed up and rode off.

He did not take the dog, who had kept well out of sight all the morning. But when he was gone, Garm slunk home and stayed there, and howled all the night, and was beaten for it, and went on howling.

"Help, ow help!" he cried. "I'll never see dear master again, and he was so terrible and splendid. I wish I had gone with him, I do."

"Shut up!" said the farmer's wife, "or you'll never live to see if he comes back or he don't."

The blacksmith heard the howls. "A bad omen," he said cheerfully.

Many days passed and no news came. "No news is bad news," he said, and burst into song.

When Farmer Giles got to court he was tired and dusty. But the knights, in polished mail and with shining helmets on their heads, were all standing by their horses. The King's summons and the inclusion of the farmer had annoyed them, and so they insisted on obeying orders literally, setting off the moment that Giles arrived. The poor farmer had barely time

55

to swallow a sop in a draught of wine before he was off on the road again. The mare was offended. What she thought of the King was luckily unexpressed, as it was highly disloyal.

It was already late in the day. "Too late in the day to start a dragon-hunt," thought Giles. But they did not go far. The knights were in no hurry, once they

had started. They rode along at their leisure, in a straggling line, knights, esquires, servants, and ponies trussed with baggage; and Farmer Giles jogging behind on his tired mare.

When evening came, they halted and pitched their tents. No provision had been made for Farmer Giles and he had to borrow what he could. The mare was indignant, and she forswore her allegiance to the house of Augustus Bonifacius.

The next day they rode on, and all the day after. On the third day they descried in the distance the dim and inhospitable mountains. Before long they were in regions where the lordship of Augustus Bonifacius was not universally acknowledged. They rode then with more care and kept closer together.

On the fourth day they reached the Wild Hills and

the borders of the dubious lands where legendary creatures were reputed to dwell. Suddenly one of those riding ahead came upon ominous footprints in the sand by a stream. They called for the farmer.

"What are these, Master Ægidius?" they said.

"Dragon-marks," said he.

"Lead on!" said they.

So now they rode west with Farmer Giles at their head, and all the rings were jingling on his leather coat. That mattered little; for all the knights were laughing and talking, and a minstrel rode with them singing a lay. Every now and again they took up the refrain of the song and sang it all together, very loud and strong. It was encouraging, for the song was good—it had been made long before in days when battles were more common than tournaments; but it was unwise. Their coming was now known to all the creatures of that land, and the dragons were cocking their ears in all the caves of the West. There was no longer any chance of their catching old Chrysophylax napping.

As luck (or the grey mare herself) would have it, when at last they drew under the very shadow of the dark mountains, Farmer Giles's mare went lame. They had now begun to ride along steep and stony paths, climbing upwards with toil and ever-growing disquiet. Bit by bit she dropped back in the line, stumbling and limping and looking so patient and sad that at last Farmer Giles was obliged to get off and walk. Soon they found themselves right at the back among the pack-ponies; but no one took any notice of them. The knights were discussing points of precedence and etiquette, and their attention was distracted. Otherwise they would have observed that dragon-marks were now obvious and numerous.

They had come, indeed, to the places where Chrysophylax often roamed, or alighted after taking his daily exercise in the air. The lower hills, and the slopes on either side of the path, had a scorched and trampled look. There was little grass, and the twisted stumps of heather and gorse stood up black amid wide patches of ash and burned earth. The region had been a dragons' playground for many a year. A dark mountain-wall loomed up before them.

Farmer Giles was concerned about his mare; but he was glad of the excuse for no longer being so conspicuous. It had not pleased him to be riding at the head of such a cavalcade in these dreary and dubious places. A little later he was gladder still, and had reason to thank his fortune (and his mare). For just about midday—it being then the Feast of Candlemas, and the seventh day of their riding—Tailbiter leaped out of its sheath, and the dragon out of his cave.

Without warning or formality he swooped out to give battle. Down he came upon them with a rush and a roar. Far from his home he had not shown himself over bold, in spite of his ancient and imperial lineage. But now he was filled with a great wrath; for he was fighting at his own gate, as it were, and with all his treasure to defend. He came round a shoulder of the mountain like a ton of thunderbolts, with a noise like a gale and a gust of red lightning.

The argument concerning precedence stopped short. All the horses shied to one side or the other, and some of the knights fell off. The ponies and the baggage and the servants turned and ran at once. They had no doubt as to the order of precedence.

Suddenly there came a rush of smoke that smothered them all, and right in the midst of it the dragon crashed into the head of the line. Several of the knights were killed before they could even issue their formal challenge to battle, and several others were bowled over, horses and all. As for the remainder, their steeds took charge of them, and turned round and fled, carrying their masters off, whether they wished it or no. Most of them wished it indeed.

But the old grey mare did not budge. Maybe she was afraid of breaking her legs on the steep stony path. Maybe she felt too tired to run away. She knew in her bones that dragons on the wing are worse behind you than before you, and you need more speed than a race-horse for flight to be useful. Besides, she had seen this Chrysophylax before, and remembered chasing him over field and brook in her own country, till he lay down tame in the village high-street. Anyway she stuck her legs out wide, and she snorted. Farmer Giles went as pale as his face could manage, but he stayed by her side; for there seemed nothing else to do.

And so it was that the dragon, charging down the line, suddenly saw straight in front of him his old enemy with Tailbiter in his hand. It was the last thing he expected. He swerved aside like a great bat and collapsed on the hillside close to the road. Up came the grey mare, quite forgetting to walk lame.

Farmer Giles, much encouraged, had scrambled hastily on her back.

"Excuse me," said he, "but were you looking for me, by any chance?"

"No indeed!" said Chrysophylax. "Who would have thought of seeing you here? I was just flying about."

"Then we meet by good luck," said Giles, "and the pleasure is mine; for I was looking for *you*. What's more, I have a bone to pick with you, several bones in a manner of speaking."

The dragon snorted. Farmer Giles put up his arm to ward off the hot gust, and with a flash Tailbiter swept forward, dangerously near the dragon's nose.

"Hey!" said he, and stopped snorting. He began to tremble and backed away, and all the fire in him was chilled. "You have not, I hope, come to kill me, good master?" he whined.

"Nay! nay!" said the farmer. "I said naught about killing." The grey mare sniffed.

"Then what, may I ask, are you doing with all these knights?" said Chrysophylax. "Knights always kill dragons, if we don't kill them first."

"I'm doing nothing with them at all. They're naught to me," said Giles. "And anyway, they are all dead now or gone. What about what you said last Epiphany?"

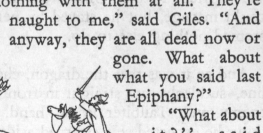

"What about it?" said the dragon anxiously.

60

"You're nigh on a month late," said Giles, "and payment is overdue. I've come to collect it. You should beg my pardon for all the bother I have been put to."

"I do indeed!" said he. "I wish you had not troubled to come."

"It'll be every bit of your treasure this time, and no market-tricks," said Giles, "or dead you'll be, and I shall hang your skin from our church steeple as a warning."

"It's cruel hard!" said the dragon.

"A bargain's a bargain," said Giles.

"Can't I keep just a ring or two, and a mite of gold, in consideration of cash payment?" said he.

"Not a brass button!" said Giles. And so they kept on for a while, chaffering and arguing like folk at a fair. Yet the end of it was as you might expect; for whatever else might be said, few had ever outlasted Farmer Giles at a bargaining.

The dragon had to walk all the way back to his cave, for Giles stuck to his side with Tailbiter held mighty close. There was a narrow path that wound up and round the mountain, and there was barely room for the two of them. The mare came just behind and she looked rather thoughtful.

It was five miles, if it was a step, and stiff going; and Giles trudged along, puffing and blowing, but never taking his eye off the worm. At last on the west side of the mountain they came to the mouth of the cave. It was large and black and forbidding, and its brazen doors swung on great pillars of iron. Plainly it had been a place of strength and pride in days long forgotten; for dragons do not build such works nor delve such mines, but dwell rather, when they may, in the tombs and treasuries of mighty men and giants of old. The doors of this deep house were set wide, and in their shadow they halted. So far Chrysophylax had had no chance to escape, but coming now to his own gate he sprang forward and prepared to plunge in.

Farmer Giles hit him with the flat of the sword. "Woa!" said he. "Before you go in, I've something to say to you. If you ain't outside again in quick time with something worth bringing, I shall come in after you and cut off your tail to begin with."

The mare sniffed. She could not imagine Farmer Giles going down alone into a dragon's den for any money on earth. But Chrysophylax was quite prepared to believe it, with Tailbiter looking so bright and sharp and all. And maybe he was right, and the mare, for all her wisdom, had not yet understood the change in her master. Farmer Giles was backing his luck, and after two encounters was beginning to fancy that no dragon could stand up to him.

Anyway, out came Chrysophylax again in mighty quick time, with twenty pounds (troy) of gold and silver, and a chest of rings and necklaces and other pretty stuff.

"There!" said he.

"Where?" said Giles. "That's not half enough, if

that's what you mean. Nor half what you've got, I'll be bound."

"Of course not!" said the dragon, rather perturbed to find that the farmer's wits seemed to have become brighter since that day in the village. "Of course not! But I can't bring it all out at once."

"Nor at twice, I'll wager," said Giles. "In you go again, and out again double quick, or I'll give you a taste of Tailbiter!"

"No!" said the dragon, and in he popped and out again double quick. "There!" said he, putting down an enormous load of gold and two chests of diamonds.

"Now try again!" said the farmer, "And try harder!"

"It's hard, cruel hard," said the dragon, as he went back in again.

But by this time the grey mare was getting a bit anxious on her own account. "Who's going to carry all this heavy stuff home, I wonder?" thought she; and she gave such a long sad look at all the bags and the boxes that the farmer guessed her mind.

"Never you worry, lass!" said he. "We'll make the old worm do the carting."

"Mercy on us!" said the dragon, who overheard these words as he came out of the cave for the third time with the biggest load of all, and a mort of rich jewels like green and red fire. "Mercy on us! If I carry all this, it will be near the death of me, and a bag more I never could manage, not if you killed me for it."

"Then there is more still, is there?" said the farmer.

"Yes," said the dragon, "enough to keep me respectable." He spoke near the truth for a rare wonder, and wisely as it turned out. "If you will leave me what remains," said he very wily, "I'll be your friend for ever. And I will carry all this treasure back to your honour's own house and not to the King's. And I will help you to keep it, what is more," said he.

Then the farmer took out a toothpick with his left hand, and he thought very hard for a minute. Then "Done with you!" he said, showing a laudable discretion. A knight would have stood out for the whole hoard and got a curse laid upon it. And as likely as not, if Giles had driven the worm to despair, he would have turned and fought in the end, Tailbiter or no Tailbiter. In which case Giles, if not slain himself, would have been obliged to slaughter his transport and leave the best part of his gains in the mountains.

Well, that was the end of it. The farmer stuffed his pockets with jewels, just in case anything went wrong; and he gave the grey mare a small load to carry. All the rest he bound on the back of Chryso-phylax in boxes and bags, till he looked like a royal pantechnicon. There was no chance of his flying, for his load was too great, and Giles had tied down his wings.

"Mighty handy this rope has turned out in the end!" he thought, and he remembered the parson with gratitude.

So off now the dragon trotted, puffing and blowing, with the mare at his tail, and the farmer holding out Caudimordax very bright and threatening. He dared try no tricks.

In spite of their burdens the mare and the dragon made better speed going back than the cavalcade had made coming. For Farmer Giles was in a hurry—not the least reason being that he had little food in his bags. Also he had no trust in Chrysophylax after his breaking of oaths so solemn and binding, and he wondered much how to get through a night without death or great loss. But before that night fell he ran again into luck; for they overtook half a dozen of the servants and ponies that had departed in haste and were now wandering at a loss in the Wild Hills. They scattered in fear and amazement, but Giles shouted after them.

"Hey, lads!" said he. "Come back! I have a job for you, and good wages while this packet lasts."

So they entered his service, being glad of a guide, and thinking that their wages might indeed come more regular now than had been usual. Then they rode on, seven men, six ponies, one mare, and a dragon; and Giles began to feel like a lord and stuck out his chest.
They halted as seldom as they could. At night Farmer Giles roped the dragon to four pickets,

one to each leg, with three men to watch him in turn. But the grey mare kept half an eye open, in case the men should try any tricks on their own account.

After three days they were back over the borders of their own country; and their arrival caused such wonder and uproar as had seldom been seen between the two seas before. In the first village that they stopped at food and drink was showered on them free, and half the young lads wanted to join in the procession. Giles chose out a dozen likely young fellows. He promised them good wages, and bought them such mounts as he could get. He was beginning to have ideas.

After resting a day he rode on again, with his new escort at his heels. They sang songs in his honour: rough and ready, but they sounded good in his ears. Some folk cheered and others laughed. It was a sight both merry and wonderful.

Soon Farmer Giles took a bend southward, and steered towards his own home, and never went near the court of the King nor sent any message. But the news of the return of Master Ægidius spread like fire from the West; and there was great astonishment and confusion. For he came hard on the heels of a royal proclamation bidding all the towns and villages to go into mourning for the fall of the brave knights in the pass of the mountains.

Wherever Giles went the mourning was cast aside, and bells were set ringing, and people thronged by the wayside shouting and waving their caps and their scarves. But they booed the poor dragon, till he began bitterly to regret the bargain he had made. It was most humiliating for one of ancient and imperial lineage. When they got back to Ham all the dogs barked at him scornfully. All except Garm: he had eyes, ears, and nose only for his master. Indeed, he went quite off his head, and turned somersaults all along the street.

Ham, of course, gave the farmer a wonderful welcome; but probably nothing pleased him more than finding the miller at a loss for a sneer and the blacksmith quite out of countenance.

"This is not the end of the affair, mark my words!" said he; but he could not think of anything worse to say and hung his head gloomily. Farmer Giles, with his six men and his dozen likely lads and the dragon and all, went on up the hill, and there they stayed quiet for a while. Only the parson was invited to the house.

The news soon reached the capital, and forgetting the official mourning, and their business as well, people gathered in the streets. There was much shouting and noise.

The King was in his great house, biting his nails and tugging his beard. Between grief and rage (and financial anxiety) his mood was so grim that no one dared speak to him. But at last the noise of the town came to his ears: it did not sound like mourning or weeping.

"What is all the noise about?" he demanded. "Tell the people to go indoors and mourn decently! It sounds more like a goose-fair."

"The dragon has come back, lord," they answered.

67

"What!" said the King. "Summon our knights, or what is left of them!"

"There is no need, lord," they answered. "With Master Ægidius behind him the dragon is tame as tame. Or so we are informed. The news has not long come in, and reports are conflicting."

"Bless our Soul!" said the King, looking greatly relieved. "And to think that we ordered a Dirge to be sung for the fellow the day after tomorrow! Cancel it! Is there any sign of our treasure?"

"Reports say that there is a veritable mountain of it, lord," they answered.

"When will it arrive?" said the King eagerly. "A good man this Ægidius—send him in to us as soon as he comes!"

There was some hesitation in replying to this. At

last someone took courage and said: "Your pardon, lord, but we hear that the farmer has turned aside towards his own home. But doubtless he will hasten here in suitable raiment at the earliest opportunity."

"Doubtless," said the King. "But confound his raiment! He had no business to go home without reporting. We are much displeased."

The earliest opportunity presented itself, and passed, and so did many later ones. In fact, Farmer Giles had been back for a good week or more, and still no word or news of him came to the court.

On the tenth day the King's rage exploded. "Send for the fellow!" he said; and they sent. It was a day's hard riding to Ham, each way.

"He will not come, lord!" said a trembling messenger two days later.

"Lightning of Heaven!" said the King. "Command him to come on Tuesday next, or he shall be cast into prison for life!"

"Your pardon, lord, but he still will not come," said a truly miserable messenger returning alone on the Tuesday.

"Ten Thousand Thunders!" said the King. "Take this fool to prison instead! Now send some men to fetch the churl in chains!" he bellowed to those that stood by.

"How many men?" they faltered. "There's a dragon, and . . . and Tailbiter, and——."

"And broomstales and fiddlesticks!" said the King. Then he ordered his white horse, and summoned his knights (or what was left of them) and a company of

men-at-arms, and he rode off in fiery anger. All the
people ran out of their houses in surprise.

But Farmer Giles had now become more than the
Hero of the Countryside: he was the Darling of the
Land; and folk did not cheer the knights and men-
at-arms as they went by, though they still took off
their hats to the King. As he drew nearer to Ham the
looks grew more sullen; in some villages the people
shut their doors and not a face could be seen.

Then the King changed from hot wrath to cold
anger. He had a grim look as he rode up at last to
the river beyond which lay Ham and the house of the
farmer. He had a mind to burn the place down. But
there was Farmer Giles on the bridge, sitting on the
grey mare with Tailbiter in his hand. No one else was
to be seen, except Garm, who was lying in the road.

"Good morning, lord!" said Giles, as cheerful as
day, not waiting to be spoken to.

The King eyed him coldly. "Your manners are
unfit for our presence," said he; "but that does not
excuse you from coming when sent for."

"I had not thought of it, lord, and that's a fact,"
said Giles. "I had matters of my own to mind, and
had wasted time enough on your errands."

"Ten Thousand Thunders!" cried the King in a
hot rage again. "To the devil with you and your
insolence! No reward will you get after this; and you
will be lucky if you escape hanging. And hanged you
shall be, unless you beg our pardon here and now,
and give us back our sword."

"Eh?" said Giles. "I have got my reward, I reckon.
Finding's keeping, and keeping's having, we say

70

here. And I reckon Tailbiter is better with me than with your folk. But what are all these knights and men for, by any chance?" he asked. "If you've come on a visit, you'd be welcome with fewer. If you want to take me away, you'll need a lot more."

The King choked, and the knights went very red and looked down their noses. Some of the men-at-arms grinned, since the King's back was turned to them.

"Give me my sword!" shouted the King, finding his voice, but forgetting his plural.

"Give us your crown!" said Giles: a staggering remark, such as had never before been heard in all the days of the Middle Kingdom.

"Lightning of Heaven! Seize him and bind him!"

cried the King, justly enraged beyond bearing. "What do you hang back for? Seize him or slay him!"

The men-at-arms strode forward.

"Help! help! help!" cried Garm.

Just at that moment the dragon got up from under the bridge. He had lain there concealed under the far bank, deep in the river. Now he let off a terrible steam, for he had drunk many gallons of water. At once there was a thick fog, and only the red eyes of the dragon to be seen in it.

"Go home, you fools!" he bellowed. "Or I will tear you to pieces. There are knights lying cold in the mountain-pass, and soon there will be more in the river. All the King's horses and all the King's men!" he roared.

Then he sprang forward and struck a claw into the King's white horse; and it galloped away like the ten thousand thunders that the King mentioned so often. The other horses followed as swiftly: some had met this dragon before and did not like the memory. The men-at-arms legged it as best they could in every direction save that of Ham.

The white horse was only scratched, and he was not allowed to go far. After a while the King brought him back. He was master of his own horse at any rate; and no one could say that he was afraid of any man or dragon on the face of the earth. The fog was gone when he got back, but so were all his knights and his men. Now things looked very different with the King all alone to talk to a stout farmer with Tailbiter and a dragon as well.

But talk did no good. Farmer Giles was obstinate.

He would not yield, and he would not fight, though the King challenged him to single combat there and then.

"Nay, lord!" said he, laughing. "Go home and get cool! I don't want to hurt you; but you had best be off, or I won't be answerable for the worm. Good day!"

And that was the end of the Battle of the Bridge of Ham. Never a penny of all the treasure did the King get, nor any word of apology from Farmer Giles, who was beginning to think mighty well of himself. What is more, from that day the power of the Middle Kingdom came to an end in that neighbourhood. For many a mile round about men took Giles for their lord. Never a man could the King with all his titles get to ride against the rebel Ægidius; for he had become the Darling of the Land, and the matter of song; and it was impossible to suppress all the lays that celebrated his deeds. The favourite one dealt with the meeting on the bridge in a hundred mock-heroic couplets.

Chrysophylax remained long in Ham, much to the profit of Giles; for the man who has a tame dragon is naturally respected. He was housed in the tithe-barn, with the leave of the parson, and there he was guarded by the twelve likely lads. In this way arose the first of the titles of Giles: Dominus de Domito Serpente, which is in the vulgar Lord of the Tame Worm, or shortly of Tame. As such he was widely honoured; but he still paid a nominal tribute to the King: six oxtails and a pint of bitter, delivered on St. Matthias' Day, that being the date of the meeting on the bridge. Before long, however, he advanced the Lord to Earl, and the belt of the Earl of Tame was indeed of great length.

After some years he became Prince Julius Ægidius and the tribute ceased. For Giles, being fabulously rich, had built himself a hall of great magnificence, and gathered great strength of men-at-arms. Very bright and gay they were, for their gear was the best that money could buy. Each of the twelve likely lads became a captain. Garm had a gold collar, and while he lived roamed at his will, a proud and happy dog, insuffer-

able to his fellows; for he expected all other dogs to accord him the respect due to the terror and splendour of his master. The grey mare passed to her days' end in peace and gave no hint of her reflections.

In the end Giles became a king, of course, the King of the Little Kingdom. He was crowned in Ham in the name of Ægidius Draconarius; but he was more often known as Old Giles Worming. For the vulgar tongue came into fashion at his court, and none of his speeches were in the Book-latin. His wife made a queen of great size and majesty, and she kept a tight hand on the household accounts. There was no getting round Queen Agatha—at least it was a long walk.

Thus Giles became at length old and venerable and had a white beard down to his knees, and a very respectable court (in which merit was often rewarded), and an entirely new order of knighthood. These were the Wormwardens, and a dragon was their ensign; the twelve likely lads were the senior members.

It must be admitted that Giles owed his rise in a large measure to luck, though he showed some wits in the use of it. Both the luck and the wits remained with him to the end of his days, to the great benefit of his friends and his neighbours. He rewarded the parson very handsomely; and even the blacksmith and the miller had their bit. For Giles could afford to be generous. But after he became king he issued a strong law against unpleasant prophecy, and made milling a royal monopoly. The blacksmith changed to the trade of an undertaker; but the miller became an obsequious servant of the crown. The parson became a bishop, and set up his see in the church of Ham, which was suitably enlarged.

Now those who live still in the lands of the Little Kingdom will observe in this history the true explanation of the names that some of its towns and villages bear in our time. For the learned in such matters inform us that Ham, being made the chief town of the new realm, by a natural confusion between the Lord of Ham and the Lord of Tame, became known by the latter name, which it retains to this day; for Thame with an *h* is a folly without warrant. Whereas in memory of the dragon, upon whom their fame and fortune were founded, the Draconarii built themselves a great house, four miles north-west of Tame, upon the spot where Giles and Chrysophylax first made acquaintance. That place became known throughout the kingdom as Aula Draconaria, or in the vulgar Worminghall, after the king's name and his standard.

The face of the land has changed since that time, and kingdoms have come and gone; woods have fallen, and rivers have shifted, and only the hills remain, and they are worn down by the rain and the wind. But still that name endures; though men now call it Wunnle (or so I am told); for villages have fallen from their pride. But in the days of which this tale speaks Worminghall it was, and a Royal Seat, and the dragon-standard flew above the trees;

and all things went well there and merrily,

while Tailbiter was above ground.

Chrysophylax begged often for his liberty; and he proved expensive to feed, since he continued to grow, as dragons will, like trees, as long as there is life in them. So it came to pass, after some years, when Giles felt himself securely established, that he let the poor worm go back home. They parted with many expressions of mutual esteem, and a pact of non-aggression upon either side. In his bad heart of hearts the dragon felt as kindly disposed towards Giles as a dragon can feel towards anyone. After all there was Tailbiter: his life might easily have been taken, and all his hoard too. As it was, he still had a mort of treasure at home in his cave (as indeed Giles suspected).

He flew back to the mountains, slowly and laboriously, for his wings were clumsy with long disuse, and his size and his armour were greatly increased. Arriving home, he at once routed out a young dragon who had had the temerity to take up residence in his cave while Chrysophylax was away. It is said that the noise of the battle was heard throughout Venedotia. When, with great satisfaction, he had devoured his defeated opponent, he felt better, and the scars of his humiliation were assuaged, and he slept for a long while. But at last, waking suddenly, he set off in search of that tallest and stupidest of the giants, who had started all the trouble one summer's night long before. He gave him a piece of his mind, and the poor fellow was very much crushed.

"A blunderbuss, was it?" said he, scratching his head. "I thought it was horseflies!"

Finis

or in the vulgar

THE END

The First (Manuscript) Version

THEN DADDY BEGAN A STORY, and this is what he said:

Once there was a giant, a fairly big giant: his walking-stick was like a tree, and his feet were very very large. If he walked down this road he would have left holes in it; if he had trodden on our garden he would have squashed it altogether; if he had bumped into our house there would have been no house left. And he might easily have bumped into it, for his head was far above the roof of it and he seldom looked where his feet were going.

Fortunately that giant lived a long way from here, a long way from anywhere where people lived. He had a big giant house among the mountains; but he had very few friends, and he used to go out walking in the hills and in the empty places at the bottom of the mountains all by himself.

One day he walked and he walked until he suddenly saw that it was getting time for supper. Then he turned round to go home, and he walked and he walked till it was dark night. And then he found out that he had lost his way, and he was in a part of the country he did not know at all. So he sat down and waited for the moon to get up. Then he walked and he walked in the moonlight, but he didn't know that he was walking and walking in the wrong direction, and getting nearer and nearer to the places where people lived, and especially to the farm of Farmer Giles, and the village called Ham.

It was a warm night, and the cows were in the fields. Farmer Giles' dog had got out, and gone off on a long walk (as he was not supposed to) all by himself. He knew that rabbits like the moonshine, but of course he had no idea that a giant was out for a walk too.

As for the giant he was now in Farmer Giles' fields trampling on hedges in a perfectly shocking fashion. The dog heard the thump-

thump as he came along the valley by the riverside, and he went over the edge of the hill to see what could be happening.

Suddenly he saw the giant step right across the river, and tread on one of the farmer's best cows, and squash the poor thing as flat as you could squash a beetle.

That was quite enough for the dog. He gave one yelp of fright and bolted home. He quite forgot that he had no business to be out at all, and he ran and barked and hollered outside Farmer Giles' bedroom window.

Out popped the head of Farmer Giles.

'Dog, what are you a-doing of?' he said.

'Nothing,' said the dog. 'But there is a giant in our fields, and he is doing dreadful things. He is stamping on your cows, and if you don't get up at once or do something very brave, you will have no hedges, and no corn, and no sheep, and no cows left.' Then the dog began to howl.

'Shut up!' said the farmer, and he shut the window. And though the night was warm, he shivered and shook. But he was very worried about his cows, and perhaps he did not believe it was really a giant, a really big giant as the dog said.

And so he went into the kitchen and took down a blunderbuss from the wall.

'What is a blunderbuss, Daddy?'

'A blunderbuss is a kind of big fat gun, with a mouth that opens wide like the end of a horn, and it goes off with a terrific bang, and sometimes it hits what you are aiming at.'

Well, Farmer Giles took down the blunderbuss, and into its wide mouth he stuffed old nails, and bits of lead, bits of broken tea-pot, and old chains, bones and stones, and lots of cotton-wool. Then he put in gun-powder at the other end, and he put on his boots and his overcoat, and went out into the garden.

He couldn't see anything but the moon shining. But he thought he could hear an awful thumping thumping coming up the hill. He remembered what his dog said, that he had got to do something very brave, so (though he did not want a little bit to be brave) he went towards the edge of the hill.

It was just at that moment that the giant's face came over the top of the hill (his feet were still far behind making havoc in the fields). The moon was in the giant's face, so he did not see the farmer. But the farmer saw him, and he was really and truly and tremendously frightened. He let off the blunderbuss without thinking – bang! He shot it right at the giant's great big ugly face, and out came the cotton-wool and the bones and stones, and the bits of chain and crock and lead and nails. Lots of them hit the giant in the face, and one nail stuck in his nose.

'Bother!' said the giant. 'Some nasty things are stinging me. There must be gnats or even horseflies in this part – really big ones or I shouldn't feel them. I don't think I will go any further this way!'

So he picked up a couple of sheep off the hillside to eat when he got home, and he turned aside, and went back up along the river. Goodness knows what happened to him after that. I suppose he must have found the way home again somehow. Anyway he didn't come to bother Farmer Giles again.

As for Farmer Giles, when the blunderbuss went off bang it knocked him over flat on his back, and there he lay looking at the moon and waiting for the giant to come and stamp on him.

The next thing he heard was people cheering. So he got up, and rubbed his head. All the people of Ham were looking out of their windows, and lots of them had put on clothes and come out on the hillside. They had heard the awful thump-thump of the giant's feet, and most of them had gone down right under the bedclothes and pulled the blankets over their heads, and some of them had got under the beds. But the farmer's dog thought a very great deal of his master, and was so frightened of him when he was angry that he couldn't imagine even a giant not being afraid of him. So now he came rushing round the village barking and hollering: 'Get up, get up! and see Farmer Giles do something very brave. Farmer Giles is going to shoot a giant for trespassing!'

And when the people and his dog saw the giant turn suddenly back and go right away, they all said that Farmer Giles had scared him, and that he would probably die of fright and the bullets of the blunderbuss, and they all started cheering.

Then they all came and shook hands with the farmer, and some of them, the parson and the miller and one or two important people, slapped him on the back. By the time Farmer Giles had had a drink, and handed drinks round to lots of other people who had done nothing to deserve it, he began to feel as brave as they said he was. By next morning he felt even braver. In a week's time he had become truly important, and the Hero of the Countryside.

At last even the king got to hear of it, and he sent a magnificent letter written in gold with a large red seal to his loyal subject and well beloved Giles, and better still he sent him a belt and a big sword.

The king had not ever used the sword himself. It belonged to his family and had been hanging in his armoury for ages. Even the king's armourer could not say how it first came there, or what its value was. So the king thought it was the very thing for a present. Heavy swords of that sort were rather old-fashioned at court just then, anyway. But Farmer Giles was immensely pleased, and his local reputation became enormous. You may be sure that no one dared to trespass on his lands after that – not any one from Ham at any rate.

So things went on for a long while – until the dragon came. In those days, although the uninhabited mountains were not so very far away, dragons were already very rare, at any rate in that country. Once they had been all too common, but the land had been famous for the bravery of the king's knights, and so many dragons got killed that they gave up coming that way. It was still the custom for Dragon's Tail to be served up at the king's Christmas Feast, and one of his knights was supposed to go out hunting on St Nicholas' day and come home with a dragon's tail not later than Christmas Eve. But for quite a long time the Royal Cook had made up an imitation Dragon's Tail of jelly and jam and almond paste with beautiful scales of icing sugar for the chief knight to carry into the hall on Christmas Eve while all the fiddlers fiddled and the trumpets rang.

That was the position of affairs when a real dragon turned up again, I don't know why. It was a hard winter that followed the summer of the giant's visit, so perhaps it was hunger.

Perhaps it was curiosity. After all the dragons on their side may have been forgetting about the knights and their swords, just as the knights were forgetting about the real dragons and getting used to imitation tails made in the kitchen. Still dragons live a long long time, and have tremendous memories. So most likely it was due to the giant. I daresay he got talking back up there in the mountains about the country down below, where there was lots and lots to eat, cows in the meadows, and sheep to be picked up off the hillside – 'if only there weren't such dreadfully stinging flies'.

Now if the dragon heard that sort of talk he would be sure to come and have a look, for dragons are not the least bit worried by flies of any kind. Come he did anyway. And he did a lot of damage, smashing and burning, and eating up cows and sheep and even horses.

He appeared first of all in a part of the country a long way off. In Farmer Giles' village people heard the news, and chattered about it quite pleasantly. 'How like old times,' they said. 'Just near Christmas too – it makes things seem quite exciting and old-fashioned.' Still the dragon went on doing damage. 'What about the king's knights?' people began to say. What about them – they did not do anything. First it appeared that the Royal Cook had already made the Dragon's Tail for Christmas so it would not do to offend him by bringing in a real tail at the last moment. He was a very valued servant. Then, when the people said 'never mind about the tail, cut his head off and stop his wicked tricks,' it turned out most unfortunately that there was a big tournament fixed for St John's Day, to which the knights of many other kingdoms were coming to compete for a great prize.

It would of course be absolutely impossible to spoil the chances of the king's knights by sending off any of them to fight dragons until the international tournament was safely over. Then came the New Year holidays. So things went on. And the Dragon came nearer and nearer to Farmer Giles' village.

One night they could see the blaze in the distance from the top of the hill. The dragon had settled in a wood about ten miles away and it was burning merrily. He was a hot dragon when he felt like it – specially after a good meal.

After that the people began to look at Farmer Giles, and it made him dreadfully uncomfortable, but he took no notice. For a day or two the dragon came some miles nearer. Then the farmer began to talk about the scandal of the king's knights, and to say that he would like to know what they were doing. 'So should we,' said the people. But the miller said: 'After all our Farmer Giles is a sort of knight. Didn't the king send him a knightly sword? Certainly he didn't dub him and say "arise Sir Giles" but he might if he were asked.' And the farmer said he wasn't worthy and was proud to be a plain honest man no better than his neighbours like the miller.

But the parson said: 'Do you have to be a knight to kill a dragon? And is not our good Giles as brave as any knight?' And all the people said 'Rather not' (to the first question) and 'Yes, hooray!' (to the second question).

And the farmer went back home very very uncomfortable, and hid the sword in a cupboard. He *had* hung it over the mantelpiece.

Then the dragon moved to the very next village. And he ate up not only sheep and cows – he ate the parson too. Then there was a terrible commotion.

All the people came up the hill headed by their parson and waited on Farmer Giles. 'We look to you,' they said. And they did, and they kept on looking till the farmer's face got as red as his waistcoat. 'When are you going to start?' they asked.

'Well I can't start today,' said he. 'I've a lot on hand with my cowman sick. I'll see about it.'

They went away. At noon the dragon moved nearer. So they came again. 'We look to you, Farmer Giles,' they said.

'Well,' said he, 'it's very awkward for me just now. My horse has gone lame, and the lambing season has started early. I'll see about it, as soon as may be'.

So they went away; all except the parson, who invited himself to dinner and said a lot of very awkward things. He asked to see the sword. When Giles brought it out of the cupboard it jumped out of the sheath, and the farmer and the parson jumped nearly out of their skins, and upset their beer.

But the parson picked it up carefully and put it back in its sheath – as far as it would go. It wouldn't go right in at all and jumped clean out again, as soon as he let go.

'Dear me,' said the parson, and took a good look at the sheath. He was a lettered man, but the farmer couldn't read even plain capitals. That's why he had never noticed the writing on the sheath. As for the king's armourer, he was so used to runes and writings on swords and sheaths he had never bothered to look at it. But the parson did. And what he saw surprised him, because he couldn't understand it. So he made a copy of it in his notebook, and after dinner he went away.

When he got home he got down lots of learned books from his shelves and sat up all night. The next day the dragon moved nearer still, and all the people shut their doors and barred their windows, and those that had cellars went down into them and sat shivering in the candlelight.

But the parson came out and went from door to door and told what he had discovered. 'Farmer Giles has the sword called Tailbiter that belonged to the greatest of all the dragon-slayers of our king's great great grandfather's day,' he said. 'It will not stay sheathed if any dragon is within a hundred miles, and without doubt in a brave man's hands no dragon can resist it.' Then some of the people put their heads out of the windows, and some came out. In the end quite a lot went up the hill with the parson, though they cast anxious looks across the river. There was no sign of the dragon. Probably he was asleep. He had been feeding very well all the Christmas time.

They hammered on the farmer's door. He came out with a very red face; he had been drinking lots of ale. Then they all began to praise him together and to call him Hero of the Countryside; and they all spoke about Tailbiter and the sword that would not be sheathed, and 'death or victory,' and the glory of the yeomanry and the backbone of the country, till the farmer got more confused than ever. So the parson explained.

Perhaps the farmer was a bit comforted when he knew his sword was Tailbiter, the very sword he had heard stories about when he was a boy. Anyway he saw that something must be done or his local reputation (which had been very nice to have) would be gone for ever. Also he had drunk a lot of ale.

Still he made one more effort to postpone the evil day. 'What!

in my old leggings and waistcoat?' he said. 'Dragon-fights need some sort of armour, from all I have heard tell. There isn't any armour in this house and that's a fact,' said he. This was a bit awkward, they all allowed. But they sent for the blacksmith. The blacksmith shook his head. 'Couldn't be done for days and days,' he said, 'and we shall all be in our graves before then,' said he, 'or leastways in the dragon.' He was a gloomy man. Then the people began to howl, and the blacksmith was quite pleased. He never even whistled at his work until some disaster (like a frost in May) had come along according to his foretelling. He was always foretelling, so sometimes it was bound to turn out as he said. However, being pleased he brightened up, and brightening up he had an idea. He made the farmer bring out a strong leather waistcoat, which he had, and he took it home and his wife put leather arms to it. And he split up all the links of the smaller chains he had lying about his forge, and he hammered them together. Then they stitched all the rings onto the leather coat till it made a sort of heavy mail jerkin. It took them a day and a half, and by that time they had made a leather mail-cap of the same sort. Then they took it to the farmer.

And now he hadn't got an excuse left to offer. So he put on top boots and an old pair of spurs, and the 'chain mail' coat, and the cap. They jingled and dingled when he walked about like a lot of Canterbury bells. But he would put on an old felt hat over the cap, and an old cloak over the mail. Probably he wanted to stop some of the jingling; it is quite unnecessary to let a dragon know you are coming along the road. Anyway he looked very funny. Then they fastened the belt and sheath round his waist, but the sword he had to carry, as it would not go back into the scabbard. He got up on to his grey mare, and very very unhappily he rode away, while all the people clapped and cheered.

He rode down the hill and across the river. And when he was well out of sight he went very slow. Very soon he passed from his own lands and came to the parts the dragon had visited. Broken trees, burned hedges and grass, and a nasty uncanny silence soon warned him of that. By now he was feeling very hot and prickly and he kept on mopping his face with a large handkerchief (not a red one; he had left that at home understanding that red rags make dragons peculiarly fierce). Still he didn't find the dragon. He rode down all sorts of lanes, and even over other farmers' deserted fields, and still he didn't find the dragon.

He was just wondering whether he hadn't done his duty and looked long enough. He was just thinking about turning back and about dinner and about telling his friends that the dragon had heard him coming and simply flown away when he turned a corner. There was the dragon lying half across a hedge with his horrible head in the middle of the road.

The grey mare sat down plop, and Farmer Giles went head first into the ditch. When he put his head out, there was the dragon wide awake looking at him.

'Good morning!' said the dragon. 'You seem surprised.'

'Good morning,' said the farmer. 'I was that!'

'Excuse me,' said the dragon, who had cocked a very suspicious ear when he heard the chink of chain-mail. 'Were you coming to kill me, by any chance?'

'Nay, nay,' said the farmer in a great hurry; and he got out of the ditch, and backed away towards his mare.

The dragon licked his lips. He was a bad dragon, as they all are, but not a very brave one (some of them aren't), and he liked meals he didn't have to fight for.

'Half a moment,' he said. 'You have dropped something.' He meant to distract the farmer's notice and then grab both man and mare and make a meal of them.

Then the farmer noticed he had dropped his sword. He picked it up, and the dragon sprang. But not as quick as Tailbiter. As soon as it was in the farmer's hand it leaped forward straight at the dragon's eyes, and it flashed in the sun.

'Ow,' said the dragon and stopped very short. 'What have you got there?'

'Only Tailbiter that was given me by the king,' said Giles.

'Oo,' said the dragon, 'I beg your pardon'. He simply lay and grovelled and the Farmer began to feel more comfortable.

'Go right away from here, you nasty pesky beast,' he began, and stepped towards the dragon waving his arms as if to shoo him away for ever back to his wicked mountains.

This was quite enough for Tailbiter. It flashed through the air and made the dragon a ringing blow right on the joint of the right wing. It hurt badly even through the scales (of course Giles knew nothing about the right way to kill dragons or it would have landed in a softer place). That was more than enough for the dragon – who could not use his wings for weeks. He got up and turned to fly. The farmer got on his mare. The dragon couldn't fly, but he could run. And he did run. So did the mare. The dragon galloped. So did the mare. And the farmer hollered and shouted, as if he was watching a horse race, and all the while he waved Tailbiter. The faster the dragon ran the more terrified he grew. The more the farmer waved Tailbiter the more confused and bewildered he became. And all the while the grey mare did her very best. On they galloped down the lanes and through the gaps in the hedges and over the fields and the brooks; and the dragon was bellowing and smoking and losing all sense of direction.

And so they crossed the river and came thundering through the village and all the people were at their windows or on the roofs, and some cheered and some laughed, and some beat tins and pans and kettles and others blew horns and whistles and the parson had the church bells rung. Such a to do and an ongoing and a racket had not been heard for years, even at fair-time.

Just outside the church the dragon gave up. He lay down in the middle of the road and gasped.

'Good people and gallant warrior,' he said as the farmer rode up, while all the folk stood at a reasonable distance with forks and pokers in their hands. 'Good people, don't kill me. I am a very very rich dragon. I will pay for all the damage. I will pay for all the people I have killed. I will give you all a really good present if you will only let me go home and fetch it.'

'How much?' said the farmer.

'Well,' said the dragon, considering – there was rather a big crowd of them – '13 and 8 each?'

'Nonsense,' said the farmer. So said they all.

'Two golden guineas each and children half-price?' said the dragon.

'Go on,' said the farmer, and so did they all.

'Ten pounds and a purse of silver for every soul?' said he.

'Kill him!' said all the people.

'A bag of gold for everybody and diamonds for the ladies?' said he.

'Now you are talking, but not good enough,' they said.

'Dear me, dear me, I shall be ruined,' he said.

'You deserve it,' said they, 'and you can choose between being ruined and slaughtered in cold blood,' they answered, drawing nearer.

Right inside him the dragon laughed, but he did not let them hear. Dragons are never fools, even when they run away. But people had had dealings with dragons very seldom lately so they were not used to all their tricks.

The dragon was getting his breath and his wits back.

'Name your own price,' he said.

Then they all began to talk at once. And the dragon sat up. But he couldn't get away, for Farmer Giles was standing by with Tailbiter, and every time the dragon moved Tailbiter made a jump towards him.

At last the parson said, 'Bring back all your ill-gotten wealth – stolen long ago I have no doubt – here to us, and we will share it fairly, and if you are very polite, and promise never to trouble this land again, we will give you back a little for yourself.'

So they let the dragon go promising to be back by Epiphany with all his wealth. One can only say it was very foolish of them.

It was then the day after New Year. Of course the king heard about it at once. And he came to the village on a white horse with many knights and trumpeters, and the people put on their best clothes and lined the street. Farmer Giles knelt before the king, and was actually patted on the back, but the knights pretended to take no notice.

Then the king explained very carefully that the dragon's wealth belonged to him as lord of all the land ('and I have no doubt,' he said, 'it was all stolen from my ancestors'). Of course he promised to see that Farmer Giles and the parson and the blacksmith should be suitably rewarded, and that everyone should have a present to show how kind he felt towards this village 'where the ancient courage of our land is still so strong,' he said. The knights were all talking about hunting each to the other.

The people bowed and curtsied and thanked him humbly – though they began to wish they had closed with the dragon's offer of ten pounds and a purse of silver all round, and kept the matter private.

Farmer Giles was the only one who was really content. He was very glad to have come out of a nasty business, and to find his local reputation higher than ever before.

The king did not go away. He pitched his pavilions in Farmer Giles' fields and waited for Epiphany. The king and his people ate up most of the bread and eggs and chickens and bacon and drank most of the old ale there was to be had in the place during the four days. But since he paid extremely well for everything ('after all,' he thought, 'I shall soon be getting all the dragon's wealth') people did not mind.

The Epiphany came, and everybody was up early. The knights put on their armour. Farmer Giles put on his coat of home-made mail (and they dared not laugh because the king would have been very angry). He also put on Tailbiter, and it went back into its sheath as easy as winking.

The parson looked a bit anxiously at it. Dinner time came. Then the afternoon – and still Tailbiter showed no signs of jumping out of the sheath and none of the watchers on the hill, nor of the little boys who had climbed to the tops of trees, could see a sign of the arrival of the dragon.

It wasn't till evening came and the stars came out that they began to suspect the dragon had never meant to come back at all. It wasn't till midnight struck and Epiphany was over, and Christmas had gone for that year, that they became really anxious.

'After all his wing was badly hurt,' said some.

But the next day and the day after passed. Then they gave up hope; and the king was very angry. The food was running short, and the knights were anxious to go back to the merriment of court. But the king wanted money.

Still back he had to go. He took his leave of his loyal subjects, but he was not so polite to Farmer Giles at going as he was in coming. 'You will hear from me later,' he said as he rode off with all his knights and trumpeters.

People thought a message would come from court to summon the farmer to the king, to be knighted at the very least. But when the message came it was quite different. The king had decided that for the safety of his realm and for the keeping of his honour and reputation the dragon must be sought out and punished for his treachery. (It was the treasure he wanted most, but he never mentioned it.) All the knights had been ordered to arm and ride out, but since his well-beloved Farmer Giles had proved himself a mighty man with dragons, and had moreover a special knowledge of this dragon and had followed him over many miles of the king's realm, it was the royal wish that Farmer Giles should ride with their company.

People said this was indeed a high honour. The miller was very envious of the farmer riding with the knights. The parson congratulated him heartily. But Giles was very upset. You can't give excuses to kings like you can to your neighbours, so lambs or no lambs, ploughing or no ploughing, milk or none, he had to get on his grey mare and go.

When Farmer Giles got to the court he found all the knights in polished mail with helmets on their heads ready on their horses. There was only time for a stirrup-cup of warm wine to be handed to him before they started off.

It was already late in the day. 'Too late to start on a dragon-hunt' thought Giles; but they rode and rode, a long line of them, knights and esquires and servants with ponies trussed with baggage, and Farmer Giles jogging along on his grey mare just behind the knights, until darkness fell. Then they pitched their tents. In this way they went on next day too until they found the tracks of the dragon. 'What are these, Farmer Giles?' they said.

'Dragon-marks,' said he.

'Lead on,' said they.

And lead on he had to. So now they rode along with Farmer Giles at the head, and all his chain rings jingling on his leather coat. The knights were laughing and talking, and a minstrel rode with them, so that every now and again they took up the refrain of a song, and sang it all together loud and strong.

It was very encouraging, and the songs were good for they had been written some time before in days when battles had been more frequent than tournaments. But it was unwise. The dragon knew about their coming long before they found his cave. There was no chance now of their catching him napping.

Now as luck would have it when at last they drew into the mountainous parts and began to ride stony tracks among the lesser hills Farmer Giles' mare grew lame – or perhaps being fond of her master (and a bit like him too) she made an excuse to get out of going at the head of a cavalcade in such very dreary dangerous-looking places.

Bit by bit the mare dropped back in the line, and nobody took any notice. There was no mistaking the dragon's tracks now. They were right in the parts where the dragon often walked or alighted from a little passage in the air. In fact all the smaller hills had a burned look about their brown tops as if these parts had been a dragon's playground for many an age. And so they had.

Glad enough Farmer Giles was not to be in so conspicuous a position any longer. And he was gladder still a little later for just before sunset on the ninth day of their riding (it then being two days from Candlemas) the Dragon leaped forth with a rush and a roar. He was not a very brave dragon far from his home but now he was very madly angry, and fighting on his own doorstep, and he couldn't run away and leave all the treasures of his cave unguarded. So fight he must, and in that case he fought like fury. And you must remember he had no idea Farmer Giles with Tailbiter was in the company. Farmer Giles was by now right at the rear jogging among the pack ponies. So he came swooping round a shoulder of mountain that hid the entrance to his cave with a noise like a gale and a blast of fire like a thunderbolt.

Everybody stopped singing. All the horses shied to one side or the other and some of the knights fell off. The ponies and the luggage turned and ran at once. Then there came a gust of smoke that smothered them all and right in the middle of it the dragon crashed into the front rank of the knights. He killed several before they could even issue their formal challenges to battle, and several more were bowled over horses and all. As for the others, the horses took charge of them and turned round and fled, carrying their masters off whether they wished it or not. Most of them wished it.

But the old grey mare never budged. She stuck her feet out wide and snorted, while Farmer Giles quaked and trembled like a jelly on her back.

The old grey mare was too tired to run away fast enough to be of any use. She knew by instinct that dragons in flight are worse behind you than before you. Besides the grey mare had seen this dragon before. She remembered chasing him over hill and dale in her own country, till he lay down tame in the village high street.

That's why the dragon suddenly saw Farmer Giles straight in front of him with Tailbiter in his hand. That was the very last thing he expected. He swerved aside like a great big bat, and collapsed on the hillside. Up came the grey mare (you really can't give the credit here to Farmer Giles). The dragon snorted. Farmer Giles put up his arm to ward off the snort (he had no shield), and out flashed Tailbiter, perilously near the dragon's nose.

'Oh!' said the dragon, and stopped snorting. He began to tremble, and he backed away. 'You have not, I hope, by any chance come to kill me, good sir,' he asked.

'Nay, nay,' said Farmer Giles (and the grey mare sniffed).

'Then what are you doing with all these knights?' said he. 'Knights always kill dragons, if the dragons don't kill them first.'

'I am doing nothing with them at all,' said Farmer Giles. 'And anyway they have all gone away – those that you have left on horseback. What about what you said you were going to do last Epiphany?'

'What about it?' said he.

'Well, it will have to be every bit of your treasure this time, and no market tricks, or dead you'll be and your skin hung from the church-steeple as a warning.' Farmer Giles was getting bolder and bolder, as he saw the dragon wobbling – it was a way he had learned at market.

'It's cruel hard,' said the dragon.

'A bargain's a bargain,' said Farmer Giles, 'and that's a fact'

'Can't I keep just a ring or two on consideration of cash payment?' said he.

'Not a brass button,' said the other – and so they kept on for a deal of a while. Yet the end of it was as you might expect: for whatever else might be said no one had ever bested Farmer Giles at bargaining. The dragon had to walk all the way back to his cave and show the grey mare the safest way up. Then Farmer Giles stood at the door and the dragon went inside.

'If you aren't outside in quick time again, I shall come in after you and cut your tail off to begin with,' said the farmer – he didn't mean it for a moment: I should like to have seen Farmer Giles going down into a dragon's hole for any money, but how was the dragon to know that, with Tailbiter looking so sharp and bright and all? So out he came again in mighty quick time with pounds and pounds of gold and silver, and a chest of rings and other pretty stuff.

'There!' said he.

'Where?' said the Farmer. 'That's not half enough – nor all you've got, I'll be bound'.

'Of course not,' said the dragon, mightily disappointed to find Farmer Giles' wits sharper than they had been that day in the village. 'But I can't bring it all out at once.'

'Nor in twice, I'll be bound,' said Farmer Giles. 'In you go again, and out again quick or I'll give you a bit of Tailbiter.'

'Oo!' said the dragon, and in he popped; and out again quick.

'There!' said he, putting down an enormous hoard of gold and silver and two chests of diamonds.

'Now try again,' said the farmer, 'and try harder.'

'It's cruel hard, cruel hard,' said the other as he went back in again.

By now the grey mare was getting a bit anxious on her own account. 'Who's going to carry all this heavy stuff home, I wonder,' thought she, and she gave such a long sad look at the bags and boxes that the farmer knew what she had in mind.

'Don't you worry, lass' said he, 'we'll make the old worm do the carting.'

'Mercy on me,' said the dragon who had overheard this last remark as he came out of the cave for the third time with the biggest load of all and the richest of the jewels. 'Mercy on me! If I carry all this it will be near the death of me, and a bag more I never could manage, not if you killed me for it,' said he.

'Then there is more still, is there,' said the Farmer.

'A bit,' said the dragon, 'enough to keep me respectable,' and he spoke the truth, probably for the first time in his life – and wisely as it turned out. 'But if you leave me that bit,' said he, very wily like, 'I will be your friend for ever; and I will take back all this to your honour's home, not to the king, and I will help you to keep it, what's more,' said he. Then the farmer took out a toothpick with his left hand and picked hard for a minute.

'Done with you,' he said – and in that he showed a truly wise discretion. Any knight would have stood out for the whole lot and as like as not would never have got it carted home, or could have had it cursed, or perhaps got the dragon so desperate that he would have fought in the end, Tailbiter or no Tailbiter.

Well, that was the end of it. The farmer stuffed all his pockets with jewels, just in case anything went wrong, and the grey mare he gave a fair load to carry. But all the rest the dragon had to shoulder, and off he trotted with the mare at his heels, and the farmer holding out Tailbiter very fierce and flashing to keep him on the straight road.

So they came home. They turned to the left at the foot of the mountains, and never went near the court of the king. But the news of them soon spread like fire. All the villages were in mourning and sorrow for the fall of the brave knights in the mountain-pass (not to mention Farmer Giles who was counted among the dead). As for the king he was biting his nails and tugging at his beard and no one dared go near him.

But soon all the bells were ringing, and people were at the road-sides singing and waving scarves as Farmer Giles rode by with the dragon as tame as tame before him. The noise of it reached the king's house.

'What's all the noise about?' said the king. 'I hope the dragon isn't coming this way. Summon my knights – or what's left of them.'

'There is no need, lord' they said. 'The dragon has returned, but tame as tame with Farmer Giles just behind.'

'Bless my soul!' said the king, looking enormously relieved. 'And to think his funeral is ordered for the day after tomorrow! When will he be here?'

There was some hesitation in answering that question. 'I fear, my lord, he has turned towards his own home,' someone said at last. 'But doubtless he will hasten here in suitable raiment at the earliest opportunity.'

'Bad manners.' said the king. 'but farmers will be farmers.'

The earliest opportunity presented itself and passed, and so did many later ones. In fact after a week still nothing was heard at court of Farmer Giles or the dragon.

'Send for the fellow,' said the king, and they sent.

'He will not come, lord,' said a trembling messenger.

'Thunder of Heaven,' said the king, 'tell him to come, or be cast into prison on Tuesday.'

'He still will not come, lord,' said a truly miserable messenger on Monday.

'Ten thousand lightnings,' said the king, 'why don't you fetch him?'

'There is Tailbiter,' said the messenger, 'and and – '

'And and fiddlesticks,' said the king, and ordered his white horse, and summoned his knights, and a troop of soldiers, and rode off in fiery anger, and all the people ran out of their houses in surprise. But Farmer Giles had become more than the Hero of the Countryside, he was the Darling of the Land, and they did not cheer the soldiers as they went by, if they still took off their hats to the king.

Very angry indeed was the king when at last he came to the river that lay between him and the lands of Farmer Giles. There was Farmer Giles sitting on the bridge on his grey mare with Tailbiter in his hand.

'Good morning, lord,' said he.

'What do you mean by it, fellow,' said the king. 'No reward will you get after this and you will be lucky to escape hanging – and that only if you come quietly and cry me pardon.'

'I have got my reward and that's a fact,' said the farmer. 'Finding's keeping and keeping's having,' said he. 'What are all these knights and soldiers for, by any chance?' he asked. 'Not to make a farmer come quietly, I should suppose.'

The king went very red and the knights looked down their noses, but certainly so many men had never gone out to fetch a farmer to court before.

'Give me your sword!' said the king.

'Give me your crown!' said the farmer – which was a staggering remark, and had never been heard from a farmer before.

'Seize him and bind him!' said the king truly and justly amazed, and some soldiers came forward. It was just at that moment that the dragon got up from under the bridge, in an awful steam, for he had been drinking gallons of water. Very soon there was a thick fog and only the red eyes of the dragon to be seen in it.

'Go home, you fools,' said the dragon, 'or I will tear you to bits. There are knights lying still in the mountain passes and soon there will be more in the river – and soldiers,' he roared. He stuck a claw into the king's white horse, and it galloped away like the ten thousand thunders the king so often mentioned. And of course all the others went after it. Not far did the white horse go for the king soon brought it back. No one could say the king was frightened of any man or dragon on the face of the earth. But if the fog was gone when he got back, so were all his knights and men; and now things looked very different with only the one king to talk to Farmer Giles with Tailbiter and a dragon.

Indeed that was the end of the Battle of the Bridge. And never a penny of all the treasure did the king get, nor any word of apology from the farmer. What's more, from that day on the old kingdom came to an end at the river, and beyond it for many a mile Farmer Giles was lord. Never a man could the king get to march against Giles, since he had become the Darling of the Land. First they called him Lord Giles of the Free Villages. But it soon became earl and later Prince, after he had built a very fine hall for himself (for he was as rich as rich) and gathered soldiers, and paid for the best armourers to fit them out well and bright.

In the end they called him King, the King beyond the River, when he was old and very venerable and had a white beard and a very respectable court. And on the whole he deserved it. Certainly he gave a good share to his neighbours, much to the parson, and a good deal to the blacksmith; and even a bit to the miller.

The family of Giles took the name of Worming from the dragon and the village of Ham was ever afterwards called Worminghall because of them. I believe you can find it still on the map, though rivers have changed since those days, and no king lives there now.

Anyway in that time it became the royal seat and the parson was its bishop, and all things went merrily and well, as long as Giles lived or his descendants after him.

As for the dragon, he was allowed to go away. And if he guessed that Farmer (I mean King) Giles had had luck on his side, he did not dare to say so. For after all there was Tailbiter – and anyway he still had a deal of treasure at home. Long after he fell in with the giant who started all the trouble getting Farmer (I mean King) Giles up in the middle of the night one June, and they came to talking about the king beyond the river.

'A blunderbuss was it,' said the giant, 'and I thought it was gnats. Maybe it was as well that I turned aside and went another way'. Anyway neither he nor any other giant ever came nigh Worminghall again. And this was at least one good reason why King Giles remained in peace and honour till his beard was five feet long.

'But who was the real hero of this story, do you suppose?' said Daddy.

'I don't know.'

'The Grey Mare, of course,' he said, and that ended it.

The Sequel

WHEN GEORGIUS DRACONARIUS (or in the vulgar young George Worming Giles' son) became King of the Little Kingdom.

George Worming was a stout young man, good with horses and dogs but not much at figures or at the Book-latin. This did not matter much since he was a King – his proper name was in fact Georgius Crassus Ægidianus Draconarius, Dominus et Comes de Domito (Serpente) Princeps de Hammo et rex totius regni (minoris). But he seldom used all that even on official documents. His people called him Our Georgie. His father was Giles (you remember), and had left him with only a small kingdom, but a fortune far exceeding that of many kings of great territory: an almost perfect situation. When he ascended the throne, or properly speaking sat in the armchair of his father he was thirty and he had two brothers [*deleted*: and Giles had married rather late and departing at length to his rest]

[*The preceding paragraph was abandoned, and the story begun again*:]

George Worming was a stout young man, good with horses and dogs but not much at figures or at the Book-latin. This did not matter much since he was a prince: his proper name was in fact Georgius Crassus Ægidianus Draconarius Princeps de Hammo (a courtesy title); but he seldom used all that. The people of the Little Kingdom called him Our Georgie. His father was King (formerly Farmer) Giles whom you may remember, and from whom he had inherited a red beard and a taste for beer. His mother was Queen Agatha, of whom he was greatly in awe – very properly and in common with all the folk of that realm (save perhaps only Giles). From her he had inherited a certain rotundity and a tenacity of purpose.

'Georgius, my lad,' said the King one day, finding Georgie in the neighbourhood of the royal stables chewing a straw. 'Well now, what's to do to-day?'

'I dunno, Father,' said Georgie. 'Things seem a bit slow-like.'

'I daresay,' said Giles. 'I like 'em slow. It costs less, and stops accidents. But there is a little matter away up north – folks seem to be complaining about these foreigners again. I had thought you might go and see how things lie.'

'I might,' said Georgie. 'Would there be any fighting?'

'Aye, there might,' said Giles. 'That'll be for you to say.'

'Aw well,' said Georgie. 'As long as I get back for our horse show, I don't mind.'

'Good lad,' said Giles. 'Now take that straw out of your mouth, and get the muck off your boots. You'd best look smart and proper, and take a few knights with you, and a banner and a trumpeter or two. Make a good impression.'

'Aw well,' said Georgie, removing the straw and looking hard at his boots. He whistled through his teeth and up came a lad, Suet.

That is how Young George came to be riding north with banner displayed and a gay troop at his back, one fine morning in May.

'Here's Georgie coming,' shouted the folk of [*the text breaks off in mid-sentence*]

*

George has a young lady up in north (choose suitable village). On his way to Farthinghoe with his retinue he turns aside to visit her. He is there captured by raiders (from Bonifacius' realm?). Treachery of lady (or her father). No news comes to Giles. George is carried off as a prisoner. ?? [*sic*] Messages pass between Giles and Boniface, but Giles refuses terms (to pay a large ransom and admit Boniface as overlord). He prepares to march forth with the Draconarii. The pig boy Suovetaurilius, popularly known as Suet, volunteers to go [*i.e.* take] a perilous message to Chrysophylax.

In the meanwhile Georgius escapes from prison, and having a marvellous way with horses either disguises himself as a horse-boy and waits opportunity, or makes friends of the King's best horse

Oxhead (or Bucephelus III) – known as Cowface. He rides away northwest because pursued. Falls in with the giant. Unfortunately he takes lodging with [the giant] Caurus, and reveals he is son of Giles. Caurus is very nasty to him. Suet reaches the Wild Hills and discovers whereabouts of George by making farmyard imitations outside all the caves (George was very fond of farmyard noises and patronized Suet at home on that account). Suet then goes off to find Chrysophylax. Difficulty in getting Chrysophylax to do anything. Long argument of Suet and the dragon. At last Suet gets Chrysophylax to go and rescue George. They tie up Caurus and stick pins into him. In meanwhile war has begun. King Giles' men are driven south, and the battle is begun near Islip. At critical moment George comes from north-west on dragon and Suet on Bucephelus. Terror falls on the Midlanders, who fly, and many are lost in the marshes of Otmoor. Extent of the Midland Kingdom, annexation of new areas West of Cherwell? Farmer Giles lives to end of his days in glory. Built dragon's castle, Suet made a lord?

In due course George succeeds [to the throne] but being disappointed in women refuses to marry and nominates Suet as his heir.

Notes

Dedication. On 5 July 1947 Tolkien wrote to Allen & Unwin about *Farmer Giles of Ham*: 'It was . . . written to order, to be read to the Lovelace Society at Worcester College. . . . For that reason I should like to put an inscription to C.H. Wilkinson on a fly-leaf, since it was Col. Wilkinson . . . who egged me to it, and has since constantly egged me to publication' (*Letters of J.R.R. Tolkien*, p. 119). Cyril Wilkinson (1888–1960) was Dean of Worcester College, Oxford, for thirty-four years. – The juxtaposition of *Wilkinson* with Pauline Baynes' drawing of the sword Tailbiter, whether by accident or intent, inevitably has been taken for a visual pun. The Wilkinson Sword company have been royal sword makers in Britain since 1772, and are renowned for the quality of their blades.

Foreword. As noted in the introduction, the mock-scholarly foreword was a late addition to *Farmer Giles of Ham* and developed through several drafts. In the first of these, 'Since Brutus came to Britain' (p. 7, third paragraph) is followed by a translation of four lines from the fourteenth-century poem *Sir Gawain and the Green Knight*, the same lines in the original Middle English, and a remark by Tolkien:

> Many strange things, strife and sadness
> At whiles in the land did fare
> And each other grief and gladness
> Oft fast have followed there.

> Where werre and wrake and wonder
> Bi sythes has wont therinne
> And oft bothe blysse and blunder
> Ful skete has skyfted sinne:

as a later historian of the reign of Arthur puts it compendiously.

The Modern English version is almost identical to the one published, as part of the complete poem, in 1975 (*Sir Gawain and the Green*

Knight, Pearl, and Sir Orfeo). In a succeeding typescript of the foreword only the Middle English version is given in the text, and a different, more literal translation is placed in a footnote:

> Where war and woe and wonder
> At times have had their day,
> And oft both bliss and blunder
> In turn have passed away.

Originally appended to these lines was the comment: 'A reference has been seen in these words to the weapon used by Giles in his first adventure, or to other similar stories. It is improbable that any reference is here intended to the first adventure of Giles or to the weapon he then used.' Tolkien changed this to read, more clearly: 'It is an attractive but improbable suggestion that *blunder* is intended as a reference to the first adventure of King Giles or to the weapon he then used. This would be the only reference in other writers concerned with early history to the legends of the Little Kingdom.' But this was not satisfactory either, and it too was refined: 'It is an attractive suggestion that *blunder* is intended to refer to the first adventure of Farmer Giles or to the weapon he then used. This is the only reference that has been discovered in other writers of early history to the legends of the Little Kingdom, and it must be admitted that it is far from certain.' Tolkien then retyped the foreword again, replacing the Middle English verse in the body of the text with his second translation and limiting the note to the revised version of the comment. It was in this form that the foreword was sent to Allen & Unwin in July 1947.

Tolkien was long concerned with *Sir Gawain and the Green Knight*. Together with E.V. Gordon he produced a standard edition (1925; second edition revised by Norman Davis, 1967), and it was the subject of his W.P. Ker Memorial Lecture in 1953 (printed in J.R.R. Tolkien, *The Monsters and the Critics and Other Essays*, 1983). In a note to Allen & Unwin which accompanied the draft foreword he identified the source of the lines he had quoted, and felt that 'they will be recognized in any case by many' – by many scholars, that is, who would also appreciate his joke in relating *blunder* 'turmoil, trouble' (so glossed in the Tolkien-Gordon edition of *Sir Gawain*) to *blunderbuss* when there is no real connection between the two words (see note for p. 15, below). In the end Tolkien chose to refer more subtly to *Sir Gawain*, reducing the verse 'Where werre and wrake and wonder' to the prose 'What with the love of petty independence on the one hand, and on the other the

greed of kings for wider realms, the years were filled with swift alternations of war and peace, of mirth and woe', 'as historians of the reign of
Arthur [e.g., the *Gawain*-poet] tell us.'

7   **a translation of this curious tale . . . dark period of the history
      of Britain.** Perhaps an allusion, one of several in the foreword,
      to the *Historia Regum Britanniae* (History of the Kings of Britain,
      c. 1135) by the Oxford cleric Geoffrey of Monmouth. Geoffrey,
      too, claimed that he was not the author of his work, but had
      translated into Latin a very ancient book written in the British
      language (a form of Celtic); whereas Tolkien presents a 'transla-
      tion' in the opposite direction, out of Latin into 'the modern
      tongue of the United Kingdom'. The Latin of the 'curious tale' is
      'insular' in that it was used in the islands (*insulae*) of Britain and
      Ireland, but also in the sense that it is debased, long removed from
      the classical tongue of Caesar and Cicero. – Geoffrey intended his
      book to illuminate a long dark period of the history of Britain,
      'dark' in the sense that no compendious history of its earliest
      rulers then existed. His account of nineteen hundred years of the
      Britons is untrustworthy as history but was hugely influential,
      notably as a major source for later writings on King Arthur.

      **Since Brutus came to Britain many kings and realms have come
      and gone. The partition under Locrin, Camber, and Albanac. . . .**
      According to Geoffrey of Monmouth (and earlier the *Historia
      Brittonum* of Nennius) Brutus was the great-grandson of Aeneas,
      the Trojan hero of Vergil's *Aeneid*. Having accidentally killed his
      father while hunting, he went into exile from Italy, gained fame
      for his military prowess, freed his fellow Trojans enslaved in
      Greece, and sailed with his people to Albion beyond the realms of
      Gaul. Brutus renamed the island *Britain* after his own name, and
      was its first ruler. On his death his three sons, Locrin, Camber,
      and Albanac, divided the kingdom between them.

8   **after the days of King Coel maybe, but before Arthur or the Seven
      Kingdoms of the English.** The mention of 'King Coel' will recall
      to most readers the nursery rhyme of Old King Cole – although
      its inspiration may have been not a king but a clothier named
      Cole-brook – which (like the two mentions of Arthur in the fore-
      word) helps to join *Farmer Giles* to traditional English literature.
      Geoffrey of Monmouth, however, alleges that Coel, Duke of

Kaelcolim or Colchester, seized the crown from King Asclepiodotus and ruled Britain for a brief period at the end of the third century. (Tolkien's friend Adam Fox, whose verse tale *Old King Coel* was published in 1937, called Geoffrey the 'most romantic and unhistorical of our historians'.) – Whether or not there was a historical King Arthur is a matter of endless dispute. Geoffrey treated him as real, giving the year of his death as 542, and it seems reasonable to assume that in referring to him here, for the purpose of establishing a date for the events of *Farmer Giles*, Tolkien is continuing to follow Geoffrey. – The term 'Seven Kingdoms of the English' (or Heptarchy) is used by some historians to refer to the kingdoms of the Angles and Saxons – Kent, Sussex, Wessex, Essex, East Anglia, Mercia, and Northumbria – in the sixth to eighth centuries.

the valley of the Thames. The River Thames rises in southern Gloucestershire and flows east through Oxfordshire, Berkshire, and London. See also note for p. 76.

The capital of the Little Kingdom was evidently, as is ours, in its south-east corner. That is, London, the capital of the United Kingdom, is in south-east England.

Otmoor. A wild moorland east of Oxford, once a great area of marshes. Cf. 'the marshes of Otmoor', p. 103.

indications in a fragmentary legend of Georgius son of Giles and his page Suovetaurilius (Suet). Tolkien's abandoned sequel to *Farmer Giles of Ham*, published in this volume. *Suovetaurilius*, see note for p. 103.

Farthingho. A village five miles east of Banbury and twenty miles north of Oxford. Also spelled *Farthinghoe*.

9 Ægidius Ahenobarbus Julius Agricola de Hammo; for people were richly endowed with names in those days. . . . Tolkien translates the Latin later in this paragraph: 'he was Farmer Giles of Ham, and he had a red beard'. Giles' 'rich endowment' of Latin names recalls the personal nomenclature of freeborn male citizens of classical Rome, which could have up to five parts (cf. *Augustus Bonifacius* etc., note for p. 20). *Ægidius* is the Latin name from which were derived French *Gilles*, English *Giles*; and the char-

acter is called *Giles* because in Britain that is a traditional generic name for a farmer, with a humorous connotation. *Ahenobarbus* means simply *red* (or *bronze*) *beard*. *Julius* is perhaps meant to be associated with *Agricola* 'farmer' in order to recall Julius Agricola (40–93), for many years a Roman military leader and governor in Britain. He was the first Roman general to effectively subdue the island, but was concerned as much with civilization as conquest. – Giles' Latin names are used variously by the people of Ham and by himself. See p. 34, where he is called 'Good Ægidius, Bold Ahenobarbus, Great Julius, Staunch Agricola', etc.; and on p. 74 he becomes temporarily 'Prince Julius Ægidius' before being crowned king as Ægidius on p. 75.

when this island was still happily divided into many kingdoms. Before the time of Athelstan in the tenth century.

vulgar form. Also 'the vulgar tongue'; the common language of a place, the vernacular. In *Farmer Giles of Ham* this is represented by English, with the exception of Welsh *Garm*. The actual vernacular in the supposed time and place of the tale would have been the British (Brythonic) variety of Celtic. – The narrator remarks on p. 9 that he 'will in what follows give the man [Giles] his name . . . in the vulgar form'; and so he does, referring to him always as English *Giles*. But the characters in the story, who are living in a past time, call him always by a Latin name, usually *Ægidius*. The passage on p. 9 is directly related to one near the end of the story, on p. 75: '[Giles] was crowned in Ham in the name of Ægidius Draconarius; but he was more often known as Old Giles Worming. For the vulgar tongue came into fashion at his court, and none of his speeches were in the Book-latin.' – Cf. *vulgar*, p. 16.

Ham was only a village. Of course, since *ham* is Old English 'village'. The word survives as a common element in English place-names.

The dog's name was Garm. In Norse mythology Garm (Garmr) is a powerful dog that guards the gates of Hel. In contrast the Garm of *Farmer Giles* is a lazy dog more interested in his own skin than in guarding his master's house. His name describes his character, whether bullying or bragging or wheedling, or yelping under Giles' window: *garm* is Welsh 'shout, cry', also recorded in Cornwall by the *English Dialect Dictionary* with the meaning 'scold, vociferate loudly'.

vernacular. See 'vulgar form' above.

Book-latin was reserved for their betters. *Book-latin* is from obsolete *Boc-leden* (Old English *bóc* 'book' + *léden* 'Latin'), 'book language', i.e. the literary language, Latin.

Garm could not talk even dog-latin. *Dog-latin* is not a language spoken by dogs, but spurious, 'mongrel' Latin.

10 **the nearest market.** In the circumscribed world of *Farmer Giles*, as in the Middle Ages and even today in Britain (though at a much reduced level), a market was held in a major town or village on a regular basis for the sale or exchange of local goods. This was an important event in the lives of ordinary people, and bound together villages in common society. Cf. *market day*, p. 19.

away west and north were the Wild Hills, and the dubious marches of the mountain-country. Cf. 'the dubious marches and the uninhabited mountains, westward and northward', p. 22. Far to the north-west of the Thames valley are the Cambrian Mountains in Wales. Later in the story Farmer Giles rides north to the King's court, then with the King's knights west to the Wild Hills to find the dragon; and on the penultimate page the dragon's home is clearly placed in Venedotia, which is north-west Wales. *Marches* are borderlands, and here 'dubious' because they were 'regions where the lordship of [the king] Augustus Bonifacius was not universally acknowledged' (p. 56).

And among other things still at large there were giants ... troublesome at times. In Geoffrey's *Historia Regum Britanniae*, when Brutus and his people came to Britain they drove the giants who were its only inhabitants into caves in the mountains. But some still roamed the land, making trouble, notably Gogmagog, who could tear up an oak tree as if it were a wand of hazel (cf. the giant in *Farmer Giles* who 'brushed elms aside like tall grasses', p. 11).

I find no mention of his name in the histories, but it does not matter. In the third (Lovelace Society) version of the story, having elaborated on the Latin name of Farmer Giles, Tolkien wrote of the giant: 'I do not recall his name, but it does not matter.' This changed to the published form *c.* July 1947, in language which refers to the foreword added at the same time.

12 **mowing-grass.** Grass reserved for mowing; hay.

13 **Galathea.** 'Goddess of milk', from Greek *gala* 'milk' + *thea* 'goddess'; see *Letters*, p. 423.

14 **sneak in the back door with the milk in the morning.** To arrive home when the milkman calls; e.g., in *The Man with Two Left Feet* by P.G. Wodehouse (1917), 'You talk of a man "going home with the milk" when you mean that he sneaks in in the small hours of the morning.'

breeches. A garment which covers the loins and thighs; a pair of short trousers.

15 **took his blunderbuss . . . used gunpowder mostly for fireworks.** The definition of *blunderbuss* (from Dutch *donder* 'thunder' + *bus* 'gun') is taken verbatim from the *Oxford English Dictionary*. The 'Four Wise Clerks of Oxenford' (after the Prologue to Chaucer's *Canterbury Tales*, 'a Clerk ther was of Oxenford', i.e. Oxford) are presumably the four editors of the *Dictionary*, James A.H. Murray, Henry Bradley, W.A. Craigie, and C.T. Onions. See also p. ix, above. – In the first version of the story Giles stuffs his blunderbuss with 'old nails, and bits of lead, bits of broken tea-pot, and old chains, bones and stones, and lots of cotton-wool. Then he put in gun-powder at the other end . . .' (p. 82).

top-boots. Hunting or riding boots with high tops.

16 **'Blast!' said the giant in his vulgar fashion.** The giant's imprecation is 'vulgar' in the sense of 'coarse'. In the drafts of *Farmer Giles* the curse progressed from 'Bother!' and 'Drat!'

away East, in the Fens. A marshy area on the east coast of England, in certain districts of Cambridgeshire, Lincolnshire, and some adjoining counties.

there were dragonflies that could bite like hot pincers. Dragonflies are sometimes known among country folk as 'devils' darning needles' or 'horse stingers', but in fact are not capable of stinging.

17   **making off about nor-nor-west.** In the direction of Wales.

18   **That will learn him!** *Learn* in the ancient sense of 'teach' is now considered archaic or slang. Cf. *Sir Gawain and the Green Knight*, 'if thou learnest him his lesson'; or Mr Badger in Kenneth Grahame's *The Wind in the Willows*, after he has had his grammar 'corrected' by the Water Rat: 'But we don't *want* to teach 'em. We want to *learn* 'em – learn 'em, learn 'em.'

    the parson, and the blacksmith, and the miller, and one or two other persons of importance. These are typical of the important figures in the life of a medieval village. The parson was responsible for its spiritual well-being, and the others were skilled craftsmen.

19   **The capital of that realm, the Middle Kingdom . . . was some twenty leagues distant from Ham.** T.A. Shippey in *The Road to Middle-earth* (1982) suggests that the capital of the Middle Kingdom is Tamworth, the ancient capital of the Mercian kings. A *league* is roughly equal to three miles.

20   **feast of St. Michael.** 29 September. It was a widespread custom, in the Middle Ages and later, to date events by the nearest festival of a saint or some other special commemoration, such as Christmas, to which the Church attached importance. Tolkien marks the progression of his story by saint's days and holidays.

    written in red upon white parchment. In the first version it is 'written in gold' (p. 84). See further, note for p. 29.

    The letter was signed with a red blot. The King probably could not write his name. Not until the twelfth century and Henry I 'Beauclerk' were the English kings held to a standard of literacy. However, the royal seal alone would have been a sufficient mark of authenticity.

    Ego Augustus Bonifacius Ambrosius Aurelianus Antoninus Pius et Magnificus, dux, rex, tyrannus, et basileus Mediterranearum Partium, subscribo. In English, this may be reduced to: 'I, Augustus Bonifacius Ambrosius Aurelianus Antoninus, virtuous and magnificent, king of the Middle Kingdom, sign below'. Like Ægidius de Hammo, the King is richly endowed with names, but they are an embarrassment of riches. *Augustus* was the surname adopted by Octavian and all subsequent Roman emperors. *Bonifacius* 'doer of good' (from Latin *bonum + facere*) is an ironic name for a king who does no good. *Ambrosius* and *Aurelianus* together recall the Roman leader of resistance against the invaders of Britain, mentioned by Gildas in his *De Excidio Britanniae* (sixth century), but also Aurelius Ambrosius, elder brother and predecessor of King Uther Pendragon and thus uncle of King Arthur, described by Geoffrey of Monmouth. *Antoninus*, finally, recalls the Roman emperor Antoninus Pius, during whose reign southern Scotland was reconquered and the Antonine Wall replaced Hadrian's wall as the northern frontier. – As if this panoply of names were not enough, the King's scribe gives him four Latin titles, each denoting 'sovereign' but with different shades of meaning. *Dux* was especially used as a title for a military commander. *Rex* is simply 'king'. *Tyrannus* refers to an absolute ruler. *Basileus* is also 'king', but with the suggestion of 'administrator'. Augustus Bonifacius, petty and ineffectual, lives up to none of them.

22 **until the dragon came.** Tolkien used similar words at the end of his 1936 British Academy lecture, *Beowulf: The Monsters and the Critics*: 'until the dragon comes'.

It was still the custom for Dragon's Tail to be served up at the King's Christmas Feast. In *Roverandom* 'dragons' tails were esteemed a great delicacy by the Saxon Kings'.

St. Nicholas' Day. 6 December.

23 **cake and almond-paste, with cunning scales of hard icing-sugar.** In the first and second versions of *Farmer Giles of Ham* the Mock Dragon's Tail was made of jelly (gelatin) and jam (thick fruit conserve) and almond paste, with icing-sugar scales. This was almost certainly devised for the young audience of those versions; in Britain jelly is a staple at children's parties. The change to *cake* was made in the version for reading to the (adult) Lovelace Society. The Mock Dragon's Tail now became, one may suppose, the fruitcake covered with marzipan that is traditional in Britain at Christmas and other festive occasions.

The chosen knight then carried this into the hall on Christmas Eve, while the fiddles played and the trumpets rang. The ornamental appearance of the Mock Tail is complemented by a theatrical presentation. Much the same occurs in the Boar's Head ceremony, still a Christmas tradition at Queen's College, Oxford and elsewhere, in which the head of a pig is carried in with much pomp.

24 **kine.** Archaic plural of *cow*.

25 **So knights are mythical.** The joke of course is that dragons are themselves mythical (or fabulous), but so are the knights in *Farmer Giles of Ham*, which are derived from popular romance.

worms. Dragons, from Old English *wyrm* 'serpent'.

Chrysophylax Dives. From Greek *krysos* 'gold' + *phylax* 'keeper', Latin *dives* 'rich'. On p. 43 the dragon introduces himself as 'Chrysophylax the Rich'.

he was of ancient and imperial lineage. Tolkien nowhere elaborates on the line of dragons to which Chrysophylax belongs; this phrase is enough to suggest an untold history. Probably it was meant to suggest no more, but inevitably one thinks of a parallel in the brood of Glórund (Glaurung), father of dragons, in Tolkien's 'Silmarillion' mythology.

He was following an engaging scent . . . slap into the tail of Chrysophylax Dives. . . . Never did a dog turn his own tail round and bolt home swifter than Garm. Cf. *Roverandom*: 'Poor old Artaxerxes drove straight up to the mouth of the Sea-serpent's cave. But he had no sooner got out of his carriage than he saw the tip of the Sea-serpent's tail sticking out of the entrance; larger it was than a row of gigantic water-barrels, and green and slimy. That was quite enough for him. He wanted to go home at once before the Worm turned again – as all worms will at odd and unexpected moments.'

27 **nosey-parker.** Someone overfond of poking his nose into the business of others.

Standing Stones. The Rollright Stones, an ancient stone circle north-west of Oxford, about thirty miles from Thame (Ham). On 5 August 1948 Tolkien wrote to Allen & Unwin about *Farmer*

Giles: 'This is a definitely located story (one of its virtues if it has any): Oxfordshire and Bucks, with a brief excursion into Wales. . . . The incident of the dog and dragon occurs near Rollright . . .' (*Letters*, p. 130).

They're queer folk in those parts. The view of a parochial villager, for whom lands only thirty miles away are foreign territory. Cf. Farmer Maggot in *The Lord of the Rings*, bk. 1, ch. 4: 'You should never have gone mixing yourself up with Hobbiton folk, Mr. Frodo. Folk are queer up there.'

worriting. Worrying.

28 **St. John's Day.** 27 December.

29 **a red letter.** The King's letter (p. 20) was entirely in red, not the usual scribal practice, which was to use red ink for decoration or for indicating, as in calendars, special events such as feast days – hence 'red-letter days'. To the miller anything in red would have been special (even if he could not read it).

dubbing. To create a knight by striking him with a sword.

30 **a plain honest man, and honest men fare ill at court, they say. It is more in your line, Master Miller.** In the medieval village the miller was the most prosperous and the least popular inhabitant, for the villagers had to bring their grain to his mill, and the miller did the measuring. He was naturally suspected of cheating, and in literature of the Middle Ages (such as *The Canterbury Tales* and *Piers Plowman*) is typically characterized as dishonest.

bosom enemies. A reversal of the phrase 'bosom friends'.

Quercetum (Oakley in the vulgar tongue). About five miles northeast of Oxford, and an equal distance north-west of Thame (Ham), thus 'the neighbouring village'. A church is recorded there as early as 1142. *Oakley* derives from Old English *ac-leah* 'oak wood'; *Quercetum* has the same meaning in Latin.

31 **Cowman.** Cowherd, one who tends cattle.

32 **He was a lettered man.** He could read and write.

uncials. A majuscule (capital) script used in manuscripts from the fourth century. In the first version of the story 'the farmer couldn't read even plain capitals' (p. 87).

There is an inscription on this sheath, and . . . epigraphical signs are visible also upon the sword. The 'archaic' characters the parson cannot read without study are presumably runes, a purely epigraphic alphabet long used in northern Europe for inscriptions on items such as coins, tools, and weapons. In *Beowulf* the sword captured by the hero and presented to Hrothgar bears a runic inscription which shows for whom it was first made. In *Farmer Giles* the King's armourer is 'accustomed to runes, names, and other signs of power and significance upon swords and scabbards'.

33 **Caudimordax, the famous sword that in popular romances is more vulgarly called Tailbiter.** The Latin name is from *cauda* 'tail' + *mordax* 'biting'. Famous weapons in literature were commonly named; cf. the sword of Thorin in *The Hobbit*, Orcrist 'goblin-cleaver', which the goblins called simply 'Biter'.

Bellomarius, the greatest of all the dragon-slayers. *Bello-* is from Latin *bellare* 'to fight'.

34 **This sword . . . will not stay sheathed, if a dragon is within five miles; and without doubt in a brave man's hands no dragon can resist it.** In the first version of *Farmer Giles* the distance is one hundred miles, which would be rather too much advance warning to the holder of the sword, and in the second version it is two miles, which would give almost no warning if the dragon were swift. – Many swords in myth and legend have special qualities. For instance, it is common that a sword could not be sheathed, once removed from its scabbard, until it had killed a man. In *The Hobbit* and *The Lord of the Rings*, elven-swords glow in the vicinity of orcs (goblins). Giles' sword, however, has inherent skill beyond that of its wielder ('Tailbiter did the best it could in inexperienced hands', p. 44).

Death or Victory, The Glory of the Yeomanry, Backbone of the Country, and the Good of one's Fellow Men. The villagers' entreaties recall recruiting slogans of the First World War. – The *Yeomanry* were men who held and cultivated their own land, and had certain privileges but were below the gentry. Tolkien noted in a letter of 5 August 1948 that Farmer Giles 'was a prosperous yeoman or franklin' (*Letters*, p. 131).

35   **leggings.** Outer coverings to protect the legs in bad weather, usually of leather or cloth and reaching from the ankle to the knee.

vulgarly known as Sunny Sam, though his proper name was Fabricius Cunctator. That is, popularly known by this nickname. His Latin name is *fabricius* 'fabricator', a maker, artificer (from Latin *faber*), a worker, especially in any hard material, such as a blacksmith + *cunctator* 'one who delays, lingers, or hesitates'.

36   **ring-mail.** Also known as *chain-mail*, a type of armour formed from interlaced metal rings, as the blacksmith says, 'with every little ring fitting into four others'.

jerkin. A close-fitting jacket or short coat, often made of leather.

skill of the dwarfs. Dwarfs in Northern mythology are renowned for their metalcraft. Cf. the dwarf-mail given by Bilbo to Frodo in *The Lord of the Rings*, bk. 2, ch. 3: 'It was close-woven of many rings, as supple almost as linen, cold as ice, and harder than steel.'

hauberks. Long coats of mail.

37   **they made him split up old chains and hammer the links into rings.** In the first version (p. 88) Giles' mail is made entirely from chains, which allows Tolkien to jokingly call it 'chain mail'. The blacksmith makes only an approximation of mail, as the rings are not interlinked but merely overlapped.

38   **Twelfthnight and the eve of the Epiphany.** Twelfth Night is 5 January, the eve of the twelfth and last day of the Christmas season. Epiphany, on 6 January, is the festival commemorating the manifestation of Christ to the Magi.

He had now no excuses left to offer; so he put on the mail jerkin and the breeches . . . and over the mail coat he threw his big grey cloak. Giles' preparation for battle is a burlesque of the elaborate arming of knights described in medieval literature, notably that of Gawain in *Sir Gawain and the Green Knight*, whose 'gilded gear' is shining and splendid. Giles in contrast cuts 'a queer figure' (p. 39).

Canterbury Bells. A reference to the small bells worn on horses that carried pilgrims to Canterbury Cathedral. The phrase, however, is actually a flower-name, genus *Campanula*, with which the pilgrims' bells are 'fancifully associated' (*Oxford English Dictionary*). The Monk in Chaucer's *Canterbury Tales* (General Prologue) has bridle-bells which jingle in a whistling wind as clear and loud as a chapel bell.

40 **came to parts that the dragon had visited. There were broken trees, burned hedges and blackened grass.** Cf. p. 58: 'The lower hills, and the slopes on either side of the path, had a scorched and trampled look. There was little grass, and the twisted stumps of heather and gorse stood up black amid wide patches of ash and burned earth.' Cf. also *The Hobbit*, ch. 11: 'The land about them grew bleak and barren. . . . There was little grass, and before long there was neither bush nor tree, and only broken and blackened stumps to speak of ones long vanished. They were come to the Desolation of the Dragon, and they were come at the waning of the year.'

red rags infuriate dragons. Tolkien extends the folklore that red-coloured cloth enrages bulls.

43 **horny old varmint.** The dragon is 'horny' by virtue of his well-armoured skin (cf. the dragon in Tolkien's poem 'The Hoard': 'His teeth were knives, and of horn his hide'). *Varmint* 'vermin, an animal of a noxious or objectionable kind' (*Oxford English Dictionary*).

44 **the grey mare put her best leg foremost.** A play on the phrase 'to put one's best foot forward', to use all possible dispatch.

45 **cenotaph.** A sepulchral monument to a deceased person whose body is elsewhere.

46 **Thirteen and eightpence.** Thirteen shillings and eight pence. In pre-decimal British currency (before 1971) one pound equalled twenty shillings, and each shilling equalled twelve pence. In the first version of the story Chrysophylax offers twelve shillings and sixpence, changed in the draft to thirteen and eight.

Two golden guineas each, and children half price. In pre-decimal British currency one guinea (originally made of gold from Guinea in West Africa) equalled twenty shillings until 1717, thereafter twenty-one shillings. 'Children half price' normally refers to a discounted price of admission; Tolkien turns it to mean that children, under this scheme, would receive only half the amount given to adults.

Now you talking. A typographical error, for 'Now you're talking', necessarily retained in this facsimile but corrected in most later editions of *Farmer Giles*.

47 **A worm won't return.** A play on the proverb 'even a worm will turn', that is, even the weakest creature will turn upon its tormentors if driven to it. See also p. 64: 'if Giles had driven the worm to despair, he would have turned....'

48 **the feast of St. Hilarius and St. Felix.** 14 January ('January the fourteenth', pp. 50–1), formerly the feast day of both St Hilarius (Hilary) of Poitiers and St Felix of Nola. The Roman calendar reform of 1969 moved the feast of St Hilary to 13 January. In the first two versions of *Farmer Giles* the dragon was chased to Ham on 2 January and 4 January respectively, and in both promised to return by Epiphany (6 January). The revised text gives Chrysophylax extra time, though even eight days is 'far too short a time for the journey', more than 150 miles to north-west Wales in each direction, and at this point the dragon could not fly with an injured wing.

He was a grammarian, and could doubtless see further into the future than others. A *grammarian* is an expert in grammar or languages in general, a philologist. However, in the Middle Ages popular belief held that grammar (chiefly Latin) included knowledge of magic and astrology. T.A. Shippey (*The Road to Middle-earth*) has suggested that Tolkien is laughing at the idea of a philologist (his own profession) having an occult ability to divine what is to come. See also p. 55, where the parson advises Giles to 'take also a long rope, for you may need it, unless my foresight deceives me.'

Ominous names.... Hilarius and Felix! I don't like the sound of them. In the third version of *Farmer Giles* the appointed date for the dragon to return to Ham was originally 'the feast of St. Hilary and St. Felix', and the gloomy blacksmith remarked only on *Felix* as an 'ominous name'. He does not like the sound of it because Latin *felix* means 'happy'. It evidently then struck

Tolkien that the Latin form of *Hilary* is *Hilarius*, which the blacksmith would connect with *hilarious*, from Latin *hilaris* 'cheerful', and naturally would dislike that name as well.

50 **suzerain.** A feudal overlord.

liege. A vassal or subject.

The knights were talking among themselves about the new fashion in hats. In the first version the knights 'were all talking about hunting each to the other' (p. 92).

pavilions. Large, stately tents.

51 **short commons.** Scanty meals.

tallies. Notched rods of wood which, until 1826, recorded sums to be paid by the English Exchequer.

Exchequer. The office or department of state charged with collecting and administering revenues; more broadly, the actual funds in the treasury.

53 **the court-hand was peculiar and as dark to the folk of Ham as the Book-latin.** *Court-hand*, in the strict use of the term, is a cursive script employed in English law-courts from the sixteenth century to the reign of George II. But here *court-hand* seems to mean merely the handwriting used in the court of Bonifacius, apparently a variety of Gothic, or blackletter. At Tolkien's request the typesetting of the two letters from the King to Farmer Giles was changed from italics to blackletter after the book was in galley proof.

54 **misdemeanours, torts, felonies, and foul perjury.** Chrysophylax is guilty of trespassing and property damage (misdemeanours), failure to return to Ham with his treasure (a *tort* or breach of duty), theft, arson, and murder (felonies), and lying under oath (perjury; 'he swore many oaths, solemn and astonishing', p. 48).

55 **no news is bad news.** To everyone but a pessimist, 'no news is good news'.

56 **sop.** A piece of bread for dipping in wine, gravy, etc. In the first version 'there was only time for a stirrup-cup of warm wine' before leaving (p. 93).

esquires. Attendants to knights; armour or shield bearers.

58   **Feast of Candlemas.** 2 February. 'The feast of the Purification of the Virgin Mary (or presentation of Christ in the Temple), celebrated with a great display of candles' (*Oxford English Dictionary*).

without warning or formality. Chrysophylax does not issue a formal challenge to battle, flouting any 'points of precedence and etiquette' the knights have been discussing (p. 57).

61   **market-tricks.** A reference to the dragon's bargaining skills when captured in Ham. Cf. p. 47: 'there was no one now living in all the realm who had had any actual experience in dealing with dragons and their tricks'.

in consideration of cash payment. Chrysophylax again lapses into modern economics. He is asking (ludicrously) for a reward for paying immediately by cash rather than on credit.

Not a brass button. Not even the smallest item of no monetary value.

chaffering and arguing like folk at a fair. *Chaffer* 'haggle, bargain'. In this sense a *fair* is a gathering for the sale of goods on a larger scale than a market (cf. note for p. 10).

62   **It was large and black and forbidding . . . the tombs and treasuries of mighty men and giants of old.** The cave of Chrysophylax recalls the Dwarf-halls of the Lonely Mountain in *The Hobbit*, occupied by Smaug, and Nargothrond in the 'Silmarillion', seized from the Elves by Glórund (Glaurung). The doors of the tower of Cirith Ungol in *The Lord of the Rings* are similarly of iron, with 'bolted brazen plates'.

I shall come in after you and cut off your tail to begin with. In the first version of this passage Giles 'didn't mean it for a moment', and the narrator adds: 'I should like to have seen Farmer Giles going down into a dragon's hole for any money' (p. 96). The second version is similar to the first; but by the third, Giles has gained self-confidence, and 'was beginning to fancy that no dragon could stand up to him'.

backing his luck. Wagering that he would succeed. Cf. the parson to Giles, pp. 54–5: 'It seems to me that you have a luck that you can trust.'

twenty pounds (troy) of gold and silver. *Troy* refers to a standard system of weights used for gems and precious metals.

63   mort. A great quantity.

64   A knight would have stood out for the whole hoard and got a curse laid on it. A notable parallel is the story in the Old Norse *Reginsmál* of the dwarf Andvari, who was caught by the god Loki in a net and had to buy himself free with his gold, to the last gold ring which Andvari then cursed.

royal pantechnicon. *Pantechnicon*, invented as the name of a bazaar of all kinds of artistic work, has come to mean a large warehouse for storing furniture, and colloquially by extension, a furniture-removal van. 'Royal' perhaps refers to the itinerant nature of royal medieval households, when vast quantities of goods had to be transported from place to place. In the second version of *Farmer Giles* Chrysophylax with the treasure tied to his back 'looked like a magnificent snail'.

Mighty handy this rope has turned out in the end. In the first version of the story the dragon carries the treasure from his cave to Ham with no intervening text (merely 'So they came home', p. 97), and no mention of how the load was secured to him. The second version was originally similar to the first, but was emended in draft so that Giles uses a rope to tie most of the treasure onto the dragon, and to bind him while travelling and at night. Not until the revisions of *c.* July 1947 was it established why Giles had conveniently brought 'a great coil of rope' (p. 55).

65   packet. A large sum of money.

66   likely young fellows. Promising, likely to succed.

67   goose-fair. A fair formerly held in many English towns around the feast of St Michael, when geese were plentiful. The allusion here is probably to the noise of fairs generally, and perhaps to the cackling of geese.

68   Dirge. A lament for the dead.

69 **broomstales and fiddlesticks!** In a word, Nonsense! A *stale* is a straight handle, thus *broomstale* 'broomstick'.

70 **Darling of the Land.** Cf. 'England's Darling', a name applied to both Alfred the Great, King of Wessex, and Hereward the Wake, who held the Isle of Ely against William the Conqueror.

71 **forgetting his plural.** A sovereign customarily refers to himself in the plural, the 'royal we', representing his subjects. The King is here so consumed by rage and greed that he forgets his proper manner of speaking, while at the same moment Giles adopts it, as he is now the *de facto* ruler of Ham and its neighbourhood.

72 **Just at that moment the dragon got up from under the bridge. . . . At once there was a thick fog, and only the red eyes of the dragon to be seen in it. . . .** Cf. Tolkien's story of Turambar and the Foalókë in *The Book of Lost Tales, Part Two* (1984, p. 97): the dragon 'sliding down the bank lay across the stream. . . . Straightway great fog and steams leapt up and a stench was mingled therein, so that that band [of men] was whelmed in vapours and well-nigh stifled . . . they fled wildly in the mists, and yet they could not discover their horses, for these in an extremity of terror broke loose and fled.'

All the King's horses and all the King's men. An allusion to the nursery rhyme 'Humpty Dumpty'.

74 **mock-heroic couplets.** Presumably a cross between *mock heroic* poetry, which burlesques epic or romantic verse (the Nun's Priest's tale in Chaucer's *Canterbury Tales* is partly mock heroic in character), and *heroic couplets*, pairs of successive lines of ten-syllable iambic verse, a form introduced into English by Chaucer in *The Legend of Good Women* (1372–86).

tithe-barn. The building in which the tithe of grain given to the parson was stored. In the Middle Ages it was a legal requirement to pay a tithe, or one-tenth, of the annual produce of the land in support of local religious establishments.

Lord of the Tame Worm, or shortly of Tame. A mock place-name etymology, and a play on the homonyms *tame* and *Thame*; see note for p. 76.

six oxtails and a pint of bitter. Items of little value. The oxtail was once considered a worthless part of the animal, to be thrown to the dogs. *Bitter* is a common kind of beer.

St. Matthias' Day. 24 February, until the Roman calendar reform of 1969.

he advanced the Lord to Earl. Giles was Lord of Tame (via 'Lord of the Tame Worm') by courtesy, and by virtue of his wealth and power; and by these qualities he advanced his own rank to Earl, then to Prince and finally King.

the belt of the Earl of Tame. A belt is granted to an earl, knight, etc. with the title. Giles' belt is 'of great length' because of his girth.

76   Wormwardens. 'Guards of the dragon'. Giles anticipates the future King Arthur by inaugurating 'an entirely new order of knighthood'.

ensign. A small heraldic flag.

But after he became king he issued a strong law against unpleasant prophecy, and made milling a royal monopoly. The blacksmith changed to the trade of an undertaker; but the miller became an obsequious servant of the crown. The blacksmith, unable to make 'unpleasant prophecy' from his anvil, takes an occupation in which death need not be foretold, and to which his gloominess well suits him. The miller would already have had a monopoly, from his lord (King Augustus Bonifacius), a typical arrangement in the Middle Ages; but King Giles having assumed authority, the miller was now subservient to his old 'bosom enemy' and became *obsequious* 'fawning, submissive'.

the true explanation of the names that some of its towns and villages bear in our time. . . . Thame with an *h* is a folly without warrant. *Thame* is pronounced *tame*, with the *h* silent, and was once so spelt. *Thame* is a 'folly' because the *h* has intruded from French into English, as also in *Thomas* and *thyme*. – Thame is a town thirteen miles east of Oxford, on and named for the river Thame, which flows into the River Thames (pronounced *tems*).

the Draconarii built themselves a great house, four miles north-west of Tame. The Draconarii are Giles (Ægidius Draconarius) and his family, the Wormings. But see note for p. 103.

77 **Aula Draconaria, or in the vulgar Worminghall.** *Aula Draconaria* 'house of the Wormings', hence *Worming* + *hall*. The village of Worminghall, some 'four miles north-west of Tame [Thame]' (p. 76), has the dialect pronunciation 'wunnle'. Its actual meaning, according to Ekwall, *Concise Oxford Dictionary of Place-names*, is '*halh* frequented by reptiles' or possibly 'Wyrma's *halh*'. Old English *halh* (*healh*) in the English Midlands seems to have meant 'nook, recess'. *Hall* 'hall, manor-house' as a place-name element is almost unknown prior to the Norman Conquest. – In the first version of *Farmer Giles* Thame does not appear; rather, 'The family of Giles took the name of Worming from the dragon and the village of Ham was ever afterwards called Worminghall because of them' (p. 100). The third version bears the subtitle 'A Legend of Worminghall'; but towards the end Tolkien writes: 'And what has all this to do with Worminghall you may ask. Very little, is the answer; but the little is this. For the learned in such matters inform us that Ham (now the chief town of the new realm)', and so forth, more or less as finally published.

Worminghall it was. That is, pronounced *worming-hall*.

Royal Seat. In this instance, the residence of the king, literally where the king sat on his throne; Thame was 'the chief town of the new realm' (p. 76).

when Tailbiter was above ground. Tolkien implies that Giles was buried with his sword.

78 **Venedotia.** Gwynnedd, i.e. north-west Wales.

84 **Dragon's Tail of jelly and jam.** See note for p. 23.

93 **stirrup-cup.** A cup handed to a man already on horseback setting out on a journey.

99 **Free Villages.** Perhaps an analogy with the Free Towns of the later Middle Ages, especially in Italy and Germany, which were free or exempt from some particular jurisdiction or lordship.

125

100 The family of Giles took the name of Worming from the dragon and the village of Ham was ever afterwards called Worminghall because of them. . . . ever came nigh Worminghall again. In the first instance of the village name Tolkien originally wrote 'Wormingham', i.e. *Worming + Ham*, then emended it to 'Worminghall', from the surname and the 'very fine hall' mentioned two paragraphs earlier. Curiously at the second instance of 'Worminghall' Tolkien first wrote that name but emended it to 'Wormingham'.

The Grey Mare, of course. Tolkien may be alluding to the proverb 'the grey mare is the better horse', which refers to a folk tale in which, a couple being presented with the choice of two horses, the wife insists upon her preference, a grey mare. Thus the proverb means 'the wife rules the husband'. In the first version of Tolkien's story Giles has no wife, but the grey mare helps to direct his actions, and shows a great deal of horse sense.

101 Georgius Crassus Ægidianus Draconarius, Dominus et Comes de Domito (Serpente) Princeps de Hammo et rex totius regni (minoris). 'George Crassus Worming, son of Giles, Lord and Count of Tame (Dragon), Prince of Ham and King of all of the Little Kingdom'. *Georgius* (George) evokes thoughts of St George, who defeated a dragon and (at least in some versions of the story) led it tame into town – although, unlike Farmer Giles, he cut off its head anyway. He was adopted as the patron saint of England by King Edward III. Latin *Crassus* 'thick, dense' suggests stupidity, Modern English 'crass'; George is not good with figures or with Latin.

courtesy title. By custom or courtesy the eldest son of a peer holding more than one title uses the title of lower rank. George is given the courtesy title *Princeps de Hammo* 'Prince of Ham', his father's title second in rank to *King* (cf. 'he became Prince Julius Ægidius', p. 74).

102 march forth with the Draconarii. Here 'Draconarii' must indicate Giles' knights (the Wormwardens, p. 76) rather than his family.

The pig boy Suovetaurilius, popularly known as Suet. That is, he cares for the pigs on Giles' farm, though he is also a general servant to George ('up came a lad, Suet', p. 102). In Roman times the *suovetaurilia* was a sacrifice, at the end of a purification ceremony, of a pig (*sus*), a sheep (*ovis*), and a bull (*taurus*). *Suet* is animal fat, used for cooking and in making tallow.

103 **Oxhead (or Bucephelus III) – known as Cowface.** The original Bucephelus was the favourite horse of Alexander the Great, named after his ox-head brandmark (Greek *bous* 'ox' + *kephale* 'head').

Caurus. Latinized from Welsh *cawr* 'giant'. In the margin of the manuscript Tolkien named the giant more fully *Caurus Maximus* 'big giant'.

farmyard imitations. A parody, perhaps, of a legendary episode in the life of King Richard I of England, when he was held captive on the continent in a location unknown to his countrymen. In one version his loyal minstrel Blondel went from castle to castle, singing a song favoured by Richard, until the king heard it and joined in, revealing his whereabouts.

stick pins into him. Unfortunately in this bare outline of the sequel Tolkien did not indicate why George and Suet would do such a thing.

Islip. A village seven miles north of Oxford.

Cherwell. The river Cherwell flows south through Oxfordshire until it reaches the river Thames at Oxford.